The Balcony at the Skyline Drive-In

North Little Rock

By
George Elda Wilson

PUBLISH AMERICA

PublishAmerica
Baltimore

First printing

At the specific preference of the author, PublishAmerica allowed this work to remain exactly as the author intended, verbatim, without editorial input.

ISBN: 1-4241-0911-6
PUBLISHED BY PUBLISHAMERICA, LLLP
www.publishamerica.com
Baltimore

Printed in the United States of America

Dedicated with Love and affection
to
Gene H. Cheatham
August 29, 1938—June 26, 2005
With out whose love, care, teaching, and consideration it
could never have been written.
And a very special thanks to Don Cheatham for his invaluable
help.

As if the already piss poor, low down rotten bad luck of being born into a poverty stricken southern family wasn't enough all by itself, I was then raised and very badly spoiled by my widowed mother and two doting sisters. Spoiled and indulged not in traditional ways, but in ways familiar to those boys brought up in southern households without the influence of a man.

Often, the women in these poor southern families, completely unknowingly, treat a lone surviving male child like some sort of a lord of a feudal manor. That was sure the case with me.

The Daddy is dead, long live his namesake!

Boys don't clean houses; girls do.

Boys don't make beds; girls do.

Boys don't cook, or do dishes; only girls do.

Momma considered it unmanly, and unseemly for a boy to do anything around the house other than occasionally carrying out the trash or mowing the lawn. This special treatment was intensified by Momma's attempt, (whether conscious or not), to keep the family name, and therefore my father alive through me.

Ours wasn't exactly what you might call a noble family name, more a mongrel than a pedigree bloodline. But my Daddy had died very unexpectedly, and still fairly young at forty-four. The fact is, if the truth be known, most of the time Momma kind of enjoyed her status as "The Widow Wilson."

"Y'all just don't know what it's like, having to raise three children on your own, without a lick of help!"

"Lordee, it's tough, havin' to be both Father and Mother to these young-uns."

"Son, you have to be the man of the house."

"Now Son, little men don't cry."

"Hush Son! Don't act like a baby."

The maternal, and sibling indulgence (forced on my sisters by Momma) allowed, no, *ensured*, that at least for my first few years I would be a whiny, pouty, pimpled, shapeless and somewhat doughy pre-adolescent brat.

Fearing rejection, and leaving the security offered by Momma's skirt-tails, I withdrew from life. Protecting myself in a tattered blanket of shyness.

Born Eliza Izora Walls, one of seven surviving children, Momma spent her childhood dirt poor. Living in isolation and poverty, on a share croppers farm just on the outskirts of a small

Arkansas town, up near the Missouri border.

The isolation had been imposed on Momma's family by her Mother Sarah, and the poverty by circumstance.

Sarah was a full-blooded Cherokee Indian who, for the first 15 years of her life lived a poor yet somewhat sheltered life with her family, within the tribe, on a reservation just outside Claremore, Oklahoma.

Until she was almost fifteen, Sarah was allowed to leave the security of the reservation for Claremore only when supplies or a white doctor were needed, then, only with her parents.

It was on one of these journeys into town that she met my white grandfather.

Headstrong, much to the dismay of her parents, Sarah had always refused to dress or act like a squaw. No silver or turquoise jewelry, or no blankets or feathers would ever be used for her adornment. Dressing and acting like she thought the white girls did, even Sarah's speech broke pattern with her heritage. She always tried real hard to sound more sophisticated, like the women she heard on the radio, and less like her family.

Standing in front of the general store, if it hadn't been for her tawny skin, you'd have thought she was just like all the other girls. Her hair had been bobbed, and her lips rouged, so anyone would have had to look real close to see that Sarah wasn't white. However, the best indication of her Indian blood, was the fact that she stood away from the other girls, talking very little, speaking only when spoken too, and then a little too slowly and precisely.

Perhaps it was because she was alone that he chose her. Perhaps it was because she was so attractive. But, more than likely it was because he recognized her as a squaw girl, and felt she would be easy pickins'.

Barely five feet tall, Sarah was slender and graceful. Her long exquisite neck supported a perfect oval face topped by jet-black hair so thick you couldn't see the scalp even where it fell away from her face. Sarah's thin sensuous lips and her huge, golden brown almond eyes were beguiling, making it almost impossible to look away.

Usually a girl this good looking wouldn't have given him a second glance. But, to the young inexperienced Indian girl the charming white man was sophisticated and very attractive. Also, perhaps a way for her to get off the reservation.

When Sarah's relationship with my grandfather was discovered, she was called in front of the Elders of the tribe. This brief inquisition led to her denunciation and immediate banishment from the reservation.

"Goddammit it to hell girl, I don't know what in the shit we're gonna do. I ain't got no money, and no job."

Sarah sat quietly, biting her lip and staring straight ahead, the silent tears making small shiny streams down her face. As bad as things were, she still hadn't told him the worst part.

He didn't know that she was pregnant! What would he do when he found out? Would he leave, or would he take her with him? Dear god, they had only done it once, how could she have gotten pregnant?

Sarah's pregnancy and finally the marriage took her and my granddaddy into the isolation that was to last the remainder of their brief lives.

Sarah died very young, barely in her mid-thirties. The untimely death could have been caused from the harshness of a life of deprivation, the rejection by her family and the tribe, or most likely, by the bearing of ten children in as many years.

Probably though, it was caused by the heartbreak of being forced to watch helplessly as two of her children died in their infancy. There had been no money for a doctor or medicine when the first little girl died from Rheumatic fever, and the next one succumbing to pneumonia. This alone would have been enough to burst all but the strongest of hearts.

Despite everything that had happened in her life, Momma had a sort of stateliness in her bearing. Not exactly like a queen or anything, but more like a refined lady from the right side of the tracks. We were certainly not from the right side, but it seemed to me like Momma always wanted folks that didn't know us to maybe think we were.

Along with Momma's careful dignity, there was also a sadness of sorts, perhaps from living a life of dreams, knowing all the while that they won't come true. There was sadness visible deep in the back of her dark brown eyes, the sort of sadness that surfaces sometimes when folks accidentally let their guard down. Without letting on, Momma always carried this sadness, and she seldom if ever let her guard down.

At one time in her life Momma had dreamed of better. Waiting, maybe for her rich uncle to get out of the poorhouse, or for her ship to come in. Finally, in despair, after seeing the end of her dreams, she now began to steel herself and us from disappointment or pain, whenever she could.

"Son, you better learn to be happy with what you got. Then you won't be disappointed when that's all you get!"

In a loving attempt to protect all of us from hurt, Momma seldom if ever allowed anyone to get close enough for us to be vulnerable. Though things seldom worked out her way, you never would have guessed it, not by the way Momma looked and acted. She held her head erect, her shoulders thrown back with her backbone straight as a ramrod, and she always appeared proud and determined, at least in public.

To make things worse, as if in defiance of her situation, Momma had always been very pretty, much like her mother. But somehow the beauty intensified her sadness. Despite the stunning coal black hair with its streak of pure white, which she proudly combed straight back from her widow's peak, and her slender (but never skinny) perfect figure, Momma was never able to completely conceal her despair.

Every other Thursday, on the day after her payday, Momma polished our shoes, starched and perfectly ironed our clothes and taking me in one hand and Neecy in the other, off we would go to town. As we walked the five blocks to downtown North Little Rock, Momma would begin paying the bills. It was always the same well-planned route, and always at almost the same time. First to Rephan's Department Store, then the NLR Water Company, and then the ARK-LA Gas Company. Momma always paid in cash, and always in person.

"If you owe somebody you ought to let them see your face every week." That's what Momma said.

Neecy and I always knew that the last stop before buying groceries was going to be the Argenta Drugstore where we'd each get a "Cherry phosphate." After the syrupy treat we'd walk the two remaining blocks to Kroger's. There, using whatever money was left from paying bills we'd buy food. We also could only buy as much as we could carry the six blocks home.

We always helped Momma put the groceries away, and afterwards there would be a special lunch of Bologna or Spam and sliced tomato sandwiches. Often followed by fig Newton's, and a glass of cold milk.

Sometimes when things seemed too over-whelming for her, or when Momma got a little bit blue, she'd escape by telling us stories of her childhood and her Mother and Father. "My Momma could make rain! Or whenever we needed a well she could always cut an old forked stick and make a divining rod."

"How'd she make it rain Momma?" asked Sister Jo.

"Let's see now! I think it was the summer I was seven when we had the worst drought you ever seen. It was so dry that whenever there was even a tiny bit of a breeze it would whip up the dust, blocking out the sun, until it was black as midnight. And Lordee, it was hot. Most of the time you'd just sit stark still, not moving a muscle and sweat would be pouring right off your face, just like a waterfall. Shoot, sometimes you'd have to put a wet rag over your face just to keep from smothering in all that dust. Ours and all our neighbor's crops, and most of the livestock were dead or dyin' and our well was runnin' dry.

Well, this one day, Maudie and me was playing in the yard when my Poppa walked out on the porch. He looked off in the distance and Maudie and me started looking at the small clouds way off in the distance that had got his attention. He walked out in the yard and the three of us stood side by side watchin' the almost invisible slivers of white hoping' they'd turn to rain."

"Lordee, kids, I sure wish I knew what it would take to make this weather turn, I don't know what's gonna happen to us if we don't get some rain soon" Poppa said, as Momma joined us in the yard. She said that when she had been just a little papoose of a girl back on the reservation, her daddy and uncle (a shaman, whatever that was) had drawn a circle on the ground, thrown some rocks into the circle and then started their rain-dance. She said that after a little while the sky started rumbling, and the lightning began to crash, and fore you knew it the rain was just a pouring down.

"It was a regular cloudburst."

"Well, why in the hell don't you do a little dancin' then?" Poppa challenged her. Then he walked across the yard, broke a limb off the cottonwood tree, and drew an almost perfect circle in the dust.

Momma's dark eyes smoldered, defiantly answering his dare. Walking slowly and deliberately across the yard she stopped, stooped over, and examined some small stones. She selected some and rejected others as she walked to the circle.

She stood perfectly still for what seemed the longest time, and finally she threw the selected pebbles across the dusty circle, studied them intently for a minute, stooped over, and picked them up and threw them again. Apparently satisfied, she began a slow tapping with first one foot and then the other, swaying back and forth in a small circle. A small rhythmic moan started in the back of her throat as her tapping grew a little faster.

The moaning grew more urgent, and you could almost make out some words. Her dancing became frenzied, and the moaning grew louder.

Slowly, and at first almost imperceptibly a tiny breeze began to cool the sweat on our faces causing fine lines of dust to dry there. The breeze grew stronger and began to wrap Momma's feed sack dress around her legs. As if possessed, a huge dust devil roared to life right in front of Momma.

The demon spiral seemed to be lifting the entire circle my Poppa had drawn right up off the ground, and you could barely make Momma out as it engulfed her in its swirling funnel of leaves, dust, debris and small stones. It tore the leaves from the cottonwood tree, scattered them onto the dusty ground, and propelled them out across the dying fields of corn.

Momma's hair was whipping around until you could hardly see her face, and, as the clouds raced across the sky and it grew darker, the first sounds of a rumbling thunder reached down to us. As if she was locked in a trance, Momma continued to dance. She stomped and whirled, moaned and cried, stooped till her hair touched the ground, and we all thought she was going to fall out for sure.

Then the lightning began.

At first, and very far away, the silver bursts now seemed to be drawn to Momma. With a huge crackle and ka-boom, a spectacular bolt reached out and struck the old cottonwood tree, shaking the ground around us. Momma seemed to be glowing blue, but she continued her frenzied dance.

The rest of us flew headlong to the shelter of the house avoiding the sparks from the cottonwood as they rained down around us. As I turned back towards Momma, she walked slowly out of the weakening cyclone.

I saw a small smile slowly appear on her face as she strolled slowly almost casually towards the house. She had just reached the shelter of the porch when the first huge drops of rain began kicking up little puffs of dust wherever they slammed into the parched thirsty ground.

Nobody ever laughed at my Momma again.

While these stories always amazed us, they seemed just a little bit farfetched. Not really like lies, but more like pleasant little dreams where nothing bad is allowed to happen. Maybe my Momma remembered them wrong, maybe not. My sisters and I always knew there had to be lots of bad…Momma was too deep down to the bone sad for there not to have been.

Momma's youngest brother Teddy, the baby of the family, developed Tuberculosis in his late teens. As the disease, always fatal in those days, ravaged unchecked and untreated through his slender fragile body consuming more and more of Teddy's breathe, he was confined to the sanitarium at Booneville, Arkansas. This was to become his home, and was where he would spend the remainder of his twenty-three years of life.

I still don't remember it, but Momma said that once, when I was just a baby, we had gone up to Booneville to see him. She also said that it was too awful to go back, what with him coughing, spitting blood and all.

The Great depression was even more severe in the farming communities of the Deep South. Arkansas had its own dust, its own bread lines, and its own misery. Poor by any standards, Momma's family was even more so during the late 20's and the early 30's.

Another of her siblings, one of her two sisters, the beautiful winsome, "Dony" was only three years older than Momma. Always longing to escape the reality of their hard life in Arkansas, "Dony" spent much of her life dreaming or looking for something, anything, better.

It was a long time before I was finally able to figure out that "Dony's" name was really *Donna*. Momma and her kin pronounced names that ended in "a" as if they ended in "y" Ida was Idy, Ava was Avy and so on and so on.

Dony spent any money she had by escaping at the flickers, often seeing the same reels over and over, or on cheap little ornaments, or makeup, hoping to attract some way out. Fascinated by wealth and fame, entranced by what she imagined was the good life to be had out west, Dony had run off to Greenville, Mississippi when she had just barely turned sixteen and married an old boy named Tyler. It seemed to her like a way of escaping.

"Lizy, he promised to take me out to California. Clean up to Hollywood. I betcha I can get into pictures or something."

The golden lure of California and the better life she imagined it offered, at first intoxicated, and then completely obsessed Dony. Spending the first months of her marriage reminding Tyler of his promise, and complaining about the harshness of life in Arkansas, she finally convinced him to leave. Hitchhiking over to Jonesboro, they caught a Trailways Bus into the hub at Little Rock, and were on their way.

Less than three weeks after Dony and Tyler arrived in Hollywood, she was found by two children on a Sunday outing with their parents in a City Park, badly beaten, Dony had been stabbed and left to die.

It was several months later when the letter arrived from the coroner in Los Angeles telling Sarah that Dony was dead, and that Tyler had committed suicide by blowing his brains out in a filling station bathroom. By the time the letter arrived Los Angeles County had already laid them both to rest in unmarked pauper's graves.

Momma always said that one of these days when she got out to California maybe she was going to find Dony's grave and get her a proper headstone.

On each side of Momma's china closet (her most prized possession) she'd hung Bronze oval picture frames with convex glass protecting the hand-tinted photographs of Dony and Teddy. The photos fading like the memories, Ted was frozen in a jaunty pose with a fedora and a bowtie. Actually, Ted looked kind of sporty in front of the English countryside backdrop with his right arm thrown casually across the artificial fence.

The picture of Dony was slowly turning translucent, and in her cream-colored lace gown she had now become pale and ghostly. Standing under a rose covered trellis, only the blue of her eyes, the pink of her cheeks and the small rose clutched gently in the fingers of her graceful hand were visible when viewed from even the slightest angle.

Their Poppa, my grandfather, had also died before I was born. Momma used to say that if her daddy had lived things would have been different. I didn't understand then, and I still don't know, exactly what events my grandfather might have been able to change, or what my Momma wished would have been different.

"Love is like a dying ember,
Only memories remain,
Through the ages I'll remember,
Blue eyes crying in the rain."

Sometimes on a summer evening, when the twilight seemed like it might last right up until morning, Momma and us would sit out on the front porch waiting for the house to cool from the heat of the day and the cooking of supper. Drinking iced tea when we had ice, or cool water directly from the tap, when we didn't, listening to the crickets and the locusts courting songs until long after darkness had finally sneaked up on us. On these precious evenings as we swung back and forth, Momma would tell us stories about her childhood (often repeating our favorites), or she'd teach us songs and the four of us would sing them together.

"Sweet and low, sweet and low, wind of the western sea.
Low, low, breathe and blow wind of the western sea.
Over the rolling waters go, come from the dying moon and blow.
One of the songs Momma liked to sing the most was:
"Farther along, we'll know all about it.
Farther along, we'll understand why.
Cheer up my brother live in the sunshine.
We'll understand it all, by and by."

"Tell us about how you could read Momma." Neecy pleaded.

"Aw sugar, you done heard that already. About a million times."

"But I like that one Momma, it makes me think of me."

"Well all right Hon, but then y'all had better go on to bed!"

"We will Momma, I promise."

"Well, this one day my Momma was out sweeping off the front

14

porch, and me and Maudie was playing in the yard, when we saw a man with a salesman's case in his hand comin' up the road. It was still pretty early in the mornin' but the heat of summer was already bearin' down on us. As he got closer we saw that the salesman was sweatin' up a river, his shirt was wet to his waist, sticking to his chest and his back."

"Leaning her broom up against the house, Momma wiped her hands on her apron, then rubbed the sweat off her cheeks and forehead with the back of her hand."

"Howdy ma'am! Boy, them is cute little girls!" the man said, noddin' at Maudie and me. "Let's see now," Momma said. "I reckon Maudie was about seven so that'd make me somewhere around four."

"Thank you kindly mister, what can I help you with?"

"Well, I'd give anything for a drink of water Maam, I'm about to smother from this heat."

Momma removed the dented tin dipper hanging on a big rusty nail on the front porch, and invited the stranger to help himself. Drawing a bucket of water from the well, he sloshed some around in the dipper and after dumping it, refilled the dipper twice, drinking heartily each time. As he returned the dipper to the post he said:

"Thank you Ma'am. I represent the Batesville Bible Company. Have you and your folks seen our wonderful new Deluxe Edition Bible?"

"Mister, I ain't got no money!"

"Well Ma'am, you don't need no money right now. For only a quarter a week you can own this lovely bible. The Batesville Bible Company will let you and your folks enjoy this wonderful Heirloom Bible with a full section devoted just to your family records."

"Not only does it have the family records section, it includes over fifty full color illustrations including two beautiful fold out pictures of Jesus kneeling in the garden, and the Last Supper."

"When he folded out the Last Supper, me and Maudie ran over to get a good look."

"Land sakes, but don't Jesus look pitiful?" Maude asked.

15

Momma said: "Now you girls go sit down and git on out of the way."

"I plopped down in the little cane rocker my daddy had made for me. Maudie just squatted right down on the edge of the porch letting, her scrawny legs dangle over the side."

"Mister, I really can't afford to buy nothin' right now."

"Well, we do have a little bit smaller Bible." he said, closing the New Deluxe edition, and laying it across my lap. "Honey, can you hold this for me?"

"Yessir"

"Lizy, don't you get that bible dirty now, you hear me?"

"Yessum."

"You can still have the full family record pages, and the complete King James Version, but the pictures ain't all in full color."

"Blessed are the poor of spirit: for theirs is the kingdom of heaven.'

"Hush now Lizy, Grownups is talkin'."

"Blessed are they that mourn: for they shall be comforted."

"I told you to hush child, you know you can't read."

"Scuse me Ma'am, but I think she is readin'. Them's the Beatitudes."

"Aw, she ain't readin' mister. She don't know how to read. She's just repeatin' somethin' she's heard somebody else say before, or somethin' she heard at church."

"Are you sure ma'am? I believe that little girls readin' for true!"

"Here honey, what's this say?" he said pointing a slender finger at the next line.

"Blessed are the meek: for they shall inherit the earth."

"She's readin', ma'am, or she's got the whole Bible memorized."

"Lordee child, where'd you learn to do that?"

"I don't know Momma."

Maudie who'd been sitting silently the whole time said:

"I showed her how Momma."

"Now Maudie, you don't know how to read neither."

And she didn't.

As Momma finished the story, only the insects and the squeaking of the porch swing as it slowly rocked us back and forth broke the silence of Second Street.

"Well Momma, how did you know how to read?" Asked Neecy.

"Oh hon, I don't rightly remember. I guess like my Momma said, I just matched up the words with the sermons from church, or with the Broadman hymnal when we'd sing."

"Now you kids go on to bed."

"Goodnight Momma, I love you."

"Goodnight kids, I love y'all too."

My Daddy's side of the family and my Momma never were able to get along with each other. Most of the time it just made things a whole lot easier on everybody, if they just stayed away from Second Street and us. In return Momma also kept us away from them as much as she could.

"Light she was, and like a fairy
And her shoes were number nine.
Herring boxes without topses,
Sandals were for Clementine"

Daddy's family were sort of rounders, if you know what I mean, just the opposite of Momma's. Momma's folks never would have shown any emotion, or discussed their lives or business with anyone other than family. And as far as I know, with the possible exception of Leroy, none of Momma's family had ever set foot in a beer joint or a honky tonk, and lord knows they never touched liquor.

Now, the Wilson's didn't have any reservations about such things. And, as if it wasn't bad enough that the men were known to be drinkers and gamblers, Mattie and the other Wilson women would hang out in the beer joints with the men folks, dancing, drinking and God knows what all.

The Wilson's didn't really seem to care even a little bit about what other folks might think of them.

Daddy's parents had both been alive when I was born. But, the bad blood between them and my Momma made them very scarce around Second Street. Both had died, (she from a burst appendix, him probably from sclerosis or some other *sin* related ailment) before I was able to begin to provide them with a permanent place in my memory.

So my little sister Neecy and I had both grown up, without ever having known the love, the luxury of being doted on, indulged, or of being spoiled rotten by our grandparents. Though Sister Jo always claimed that she remembered them, I never knew if she really did, or if it was just something else that she made up.

Daddy's older brother Joe and his family lived in a squatter's camp down towards Rose City, right on the Arkansas River. Just across the levee, the camp sat smack-dab right on the river's bank. It really wasn't anything more than just a big old army tent with wood floors. But, it was home to Joe, Jessie and their five red-haired, freckle faced boys.

Occasionally, the lean accommodations found on the River bank also became home to several old mixed breed hound dogs, and one or two scraggly cows, which Joe usually kept tied up to the outhouse. Really just two walls on the sides and a front door under a lean-to roof, the outhouse backed up to a stand of saplings, so Joe had seen no reason to protect the backsides of the users.

Frequently there might be some talk about building a fence, but what with hunting, drinking and resting, Joe and them were way too busy or plumb wore out for that.

Every few years the whole mess, sometimes even the livestock got washed away by a rampaging Arkansas River. During these frequent spring floods the town would shut the floodgates, and Joe and Jessie would evacuate the entire brood across the levee, and over to Mattie and Lloyd's place.

Mattie, Daddy's oldest sister, lived with her husband Lloyd and their daughters Jewel and Nadine in one side of a small duplex just off East Third Street. From there, it was just a few blocks walk to downtown North Little Rock, and the Star Cafe where Lloyd worked as a cook.

Sometimes when Daddy was feeling real flush he'd take us down to the Star for a plate lunch or a piece of pie. On these infrequent trips, Uncle Lloyd would always give us a little somethin' extra. With a sly little wink to Sister Jo, or me Lloyd would dab on an extra spoonful of stew or dumplin's until our plates were almost overflowing. And of course, there was never ever any charge for pie or banana pudding at the Star cafe.

Anytime Daddy got with Mattie, or Joe and them, he'd get all tanked up. Then Momma and us generally wouldn't lay eyes on him till he'd blown his whole paycheck. Usually he'd come dragging in late on a Sunday night, always remorseful, usually broke, and more than a little hung-over. The stale smell of beer, cigarettes and other women would be clinging to him like some cheap after-shave. Whenever this happened, him and Momma would get into a knockdown drag-out fight, and Sister Jo would take me and Neecy out on the porch, where we'd swing real hard and sing real loud, trying not to hear the commotion.

One of Daddy's, and the Wilson's favorite hangouts, was the Bridge Tavern at First and Main. Well, it was really just the second floor of a shabby, all but deserted, old red brick building. You entered the tavern by walking right off the Main Street Bridge.

You just walked across a little catwalk and there you were right inside the beer joint. Momma thought it was trashy, but I kinda liked it. There was a long bar on the left when you entered, and the only other furnishings were a few uncovered tables, some rickety chairs, and a jukebox.

Usually anytime we went into the place "Old Hank" was usually singing something about a "Honky-Tonk Angel" or that old wooden Indian "Kawliga."

On the bottom floor, directly under the Tavern, was a little barbershop. Daddy'd take me there when it was time to get our haircuts. To get into the Barber Shop, customers had to double back, and cross under the bridge. Because of the cutting instruments and the smell of alcohol I was always a little bit frightened, but also fascinated by the Barber Shop.

In the corner by the front window there was a small metal shelf which held a small teardrop shaped plastic bird beside a huge can of talcum. The little bird had a real feather tail, and rocked constantly back and forth until every few swings it leaned completely over and stuck it's beak in a glass of water sat there just for that purpose.

Strangely enough, the Barber Shop's pole was on the second floor, just outside the entrance to the tavern.

One of the worst fights Daddy and Momma ever had was the time he took me and Sister Jo to the Bridge Tavern, and we stayed the whole day right into the evening. Sister Jo spent the day playing dominos with Mattie and Jessie while I showed off in my navy and white sailor suit.

As I walked up and down on the top of the bar, folk's were giving me their change, egging me on to dance to the music from the jukebox or to sing a little bit of one song or another.

"I'm walking the floor over you.
I can't sleep a wink that is true..."

Like my Momma, Daddy was also real good looking. Everybody always said they made a very handsome couple.

Tall and lanky, Daddy always wore a white shirt rolled back at the cuffs, and a hat that he'd pushed way back on his head so's his hair could show. In every picture you ever saw of my daddy, he always had a cigarette, either in his slender hand or held between his full lips. The cigarettes were self-rolled by him or Sister Jo, on a little machine kept on a shelf over the cook stove.

The small tin cigarette roller was painted green, and had a large red rubber strip. On which, after licking the gummed strip on the paper you'd make a little paper bed at one end. After pushing the paper down with your fingertip, gently, so as not to tear the thin paper, you filled the small depression with tobacco from the grayish white cotton drawstring bag, and cranked the handle. Then, as if by puredee magic, out of the other end rolled a perfect little cigarette.

When Sister Jo and Daddy got a bunch all made up, Daddy'd carefully line them up in the old tin Camel can he always carried in his shirt pocket. That way, nobody would know that he was smoking home-rolled.

My Daddy was considered to be quite a charmer and a ladies man.

Many years after he died, Momma still kept among her memories an old square powder can. Of pale blue enamel, the small slender can had been painted with little white lilies of the valley, and was permanently bent into a semicircle from the curve of Daddy's head where Momma had hit him with it while attempting to defend herself.

"Goddammit-it Eldy (the Wilson's always called Daddy by his middle name), I'm tellin' you, we can make a shit-pile full of cash if you'll only throw in with us."

It was Sunday, and Daddy had taken me with him over to Joe's and Jessie's to eat supper, and for the two of them to get likkered up and shoot the bull. When Joe wasn't plannin' some get rich quick scheme, he was tryin' to figure out a way to sue somebody for something, like an injury, real or otherwise.

"Joe, I ain't got no money. But even if I did, Lizy would kill me if she ever was to find out I gave any of what little we got to you."

Jessie was standing over in the corner, frying pork-chops on an old wood stove. Trying hard to keep from burning herself with the splattering grease and to hear what the two men were saying.

"Shoot George, you'd have the money back soon as Joe got the first load of wood sold."

She was a real good cook. And, if you didn't think about where it came from for too long, you could really enjoy one of her meals.

The tent wasn't really divided up into what you might call rooms. Curtains or large pieces of rundown furniture separated the olive drab canopy into different areas for cooking, or for sitting, or sleeping. There was only one bedstead in the whole place, and that was for Jessie and Joe. The boys all slept on pallets or featherbeds which were just thrown onto the wooden floor every night. The floor, if you could call it that, was just some old rough unfinished logs that Joe had cut in half lengthwise, then him and the boys laid them side by side without even nailing them together, directly onto the ground, flat side up.

"Hell Eldy, the county won't give a shit if we chop down a few old trees and sell the wood. I'm tellin' you we can do all right."

"What do you want me to do Joe?"

"We need seventy five dollars to buy a wagon for my mule. Then I'll be able to peddle the wood through some of them fancy neighborhoods like Pulaski Heights or Park Hill."

Well, daddy got the money from somewhere (I suspect from one or two of his women friends), and Joe got arrested the very first day for taking timber from public land. The judge only gave Joe a few days at the county farm, but he had gotten a free wagon for his trouble. I suppose my daddy was able to figure out some way to pay the woman back.

Aunt Maude was Momma's older and only surviving sister. A not quite so attractive version of Momma, Maude was married to my kind, generous and long suffering Uncle Arthur. Aunt Maude and Uncle Arthur lived on East Second Street, just a few blocks away from us, and just a block over on the next street from Mattie and Lloyd. It might as well have been the other side of the moon though. For, as far as I know, neither woman would ever have dreamed of setting foot in the other's house.

Momma would say (very disapprovingly), she'd get that look on her face. That sometimes, when Uncle Arthur would get a little nervous he would take a drink or two. I don't know about all that, but as far as us kids were concerned, he was just a very friendly, somewhat over-grown playmate. Usually smelling of sawdust and Sen-Sen, Uncle Arthur was always able to find a penny in his pocket or a package of Dentyne for Neecy, Sister Jo and me.

Other than Maude, Momma's remaining siblings included the once fastidious Willie, who shocked his family when at twenty-three he became smitten with, and then married the slovenly Hattie. Willie and Hattie, along with their eleven kids (some of which didn't seem quite right), eked a measly living off a sharecropper's farm, on the outskirts of Bald Knob, Arkansas.

Somehow, Momma's oldest brother Roland had risen above his humble beginnings. And, was now a circuit judge up in White River County.

We never did know Roland, and we met the other brother, Fate, only once. Fate was the postmaster in Gid, Arkansas, and a year or two before Momma married J.W. we'd gone up there for Decoration Day.

It was a small ramshackle country church and cemetery. The congregation had spread sheets over the long plank tables under the big old elm trees, and placed a spectacular array of food on them. There was everything from Chicken and dumplings, to boiled beef and noodles, and every kind of pie or cake you had ever heard of. I don't know who's graves they were, but us littler kids ran and played among the tombstones, stopping every now and then for just long enough to grab another piece of fried chicken or peach pie. Through all this the adults and bigger kids cleaned the cemetery.

Then there was the youngest brother, Leroy. Leroy, like us lived in North Little Rock. Well, sort of. Leroy never did work! And, as far as I know, he never had a regular place to live either. Unless, you counted hanging out with the other hobos under one of the several bridges that crossed the Arkansas River, or wherever he had passed out along the levee or on the river bank as a place.

The most frequent, and certainly the nicest place Leroy ever lived was the County farm. When for several months each winter he became a resident. Sometimes, I suspect this confinement was voluntary. Each year as cooler weather began its approach Leroy would begin looking for some sort of minor offense to commit, in order to get arrested before the really bad weather arrived. Crapping in the lobby of the police station, or pissing on an officer's leg, was just two of his favorite ways to secure a winter's berth at the County farm.

The North Little Rock police, along with the other hobos, and sometimes, even Leroy himself, used several names when referring to my uncle. "Poor boy Roy" and "Roy Boy" are two that I remember.

After Leroy would succeed in his effort to get arrested, and as soon as he sobered up, the deputies at the County farm always made him a trustee. According to Momma he was a very good worker, at least when he wasn't drunk. However, where Leroy was concerned a little bit of close supervision was a very good idea.

Once, after he had driven a county truck into Little Rock to pick up the months supplies, he didn't return for several days. It seems that while he had been gone, ol "Poor boy Roy" had traded several of the more important engine parts to some unscrupulous mechanic. He'd earned enough money to finance a three-day drunk for him, and for several of his cronies.

When the deputies finally did catch him, the judge graciously decided to extend his stay at the County farm several additional months. The deputies told Momma that "Ole Poor boy Roy" didn't seem at all upset with the sentence, what with winter coming on and all.

Leroy's drink of choice was most often cheap muscatel wine. But, when times got tough, and he was allowed into someone's house or gained access to a bathroom medicine cabinet, he was known to guzzle shaving lotion, cough syrup, or even "canned heat" after it had been strained through whatever cloth was available (a dirty rag, or an old "tee" shirt, would work). I know of one occasion when he had stepped right out of his underwear and squeezed a can of the pink gel right through them, to make this concoction. After straining the gelatinous red fuel, the biting red syrup was then poured into a used wine bottle.

There, it was mixed with equal parts of water from one of the many barrels catching rain on the Baring Cross Railroad Bridge. Leroy said it was "Pretty good drinkin', if you don't mind the trots."

Oh now, don't get me wrong. Maudie and Momma really did love their little brother.

But, both of Leroy's sisters had learned from past experiences never to lend him money, allow him to stay overnight, or even to let him come inside their houses when he was drinking.

Whenever he came by begging for money or food, they'd sometimes give him a plate of leftovers. These had to be eaten on the front porch or out in the yard.

One cold January night, so the story went, a very young Leroy and his wife awakened from their drunken stupors, to find that their only child had been suffocated by the bedcovers. They say that until that time, Leroy had held down a regular job at the mill in Cotton Plant, Arkansas. At least, that's the explanation Maudie or Momma would give anytime an excuse for his behavior seemed to be called for.

Eventually though, perhaps from the guilt, he and the wife separated, and he lost his job at the mill. Never working at a regular job again, Leroy would sometimes do part-time work at the labor pool whenever he was sober enough, and then, only for as long as it took to finance his next drunk.

Momma had been sick in bed the day my daddy died. Some said that she had a stroke. But, most likely it was a reaction to some dental work. The dentist (probably selected because of price or maybe because he'd let them pay on time) had pulled almost all of her teeth at one time.

"Sister Jo" had taken "Neecy and me" to the picture show that day. I had just recently turned four and "Neecy" was just barely out of her infancy, so "Sister Jo" had really had her hands full.

After the picture show "Sister Jo," with the extra money daddy had given her bought each of us a ball fringe cowboy hat (The kind Zorro wore) from the five and dime.

The day was unusual for several reasons—the amount of the money Daddy had given us, and the fact that he'd had it to give to us in the first place. And, because in the early afternoon, Daddy, (while walking to the Bridge Tavern with his brother Joe) stepped off the curb and dropped, already dead, of a heart attack, while my sisters and I were at the Princess Theater being thrilled by the exploits of Lash Larue, Whip Wilson or Bob Steele.

He had only just recently had his forty-fourth birthday.

Unable to leave her bed, Momma stayed at home while we kids were taken to Daddy's funeral by Aunt Maude and Uncle Arthur. Immediately following the funeral Mattie and the rest had come straight to the house and carried out all Daddy's personal belongings. Not a single one of the Wilson's ever returned to our house until I was almost grown. It now fell entirely on Maude and Arthur to help out, and help Momma take care of us kids.

We had always been close to Maud and Arthur, but after my

daddy died, they both, especially Uncle Arthur, took us kids as their own personal responsibility. Childless, both of them had always doted on us, but now they became self-appointed substitute parents. Maude, unlike Arthur saw herself as an authority figure. But dear gentle Uncle Arthur wanted only to be our friend and protector.

Arthur's hands were incredible, so huge he could cover the entire top of mine or Neecy's head with just one pat. Calloused and scarred they looked frightful yet they were as gentle as an angel's touch. Seeing him coming down the sidewalk, we'd fly off the porch. Running to meet him in breathless anticipation of feeling those large loving hands on our heads. Then slowly walking beside him back up to the house. Way over six feet tall, and tipping the scale at two hundred pounds, this giant man intimidated most folks, but to us kids his size went unnoticed because of his gentleness. Second Street had now become my Uncle Arthur's first stop on his long walk home from the excelsior plant.

I never did understand exactly what they made at the excelsior plant, but I do remember that he ran some sort of a huge saw or a grinding machine, standing and feeding wood into it for eight hours a day. Always covered from head to toe with the fine dust, even the shine of his baldhead was dulled by the sticky residue of excelsior. Arriving at our back porch nearly every day of the week, he usually wouldn't come inside for fear of arousing Momma's ire by tracking up her kitchen.

Sitting down on the edge of the porch, Arthur would begin fishing in his overall pockets or the almost empty lunch pail. Finally he would produce whatever our treat of the day was to be, depending on how many pennies he had been able to hide from Maude.

Aunt Maude was very frugal, at least when it came to sharing Arthur's meager salary with Arthur. However, her generosity knew no bounds wherever Maude was concerned. After rent, food, and fifty cents a week to the funeral home, the remainder of his meager earnings went for bedspreads, curtains, chenille robes, Tiddly Winks games for us kids, or whatever else the L.B. Price, Standard Coffee or Jewel Tea trucks had to offer.

26

These door-to-door vendors crisscrossed the neighborhoods of the poor or almost poor like shiny four wheeled vultures. They fascinated the residents with items guaranteed to make their lives better or easier, and more like the rich folks living in mansions on the hills above North Little Rock. And best of all...they sold on time.

Now, As far as I was concerned, west Second Street might just as well have been the entire universe. We had always been, or so it seemed to me, to be tethered to the old gray frame house with its peeling paint, and its tarpaper roof. Standing forlornly on the corner of Second and Elm Street, the little house had been built long before there was indoor plumbing. Sometime before we had moved in, someone had thoughtfully added a flush toilet and a bathtub in the small room just across the open back porch. Leaving the warmth of the kitchen, after holding it in as long as we could, we'd spring across the porch to the bathroom, sometimes only just barely making it.

There was no hot water of course. But, when it was needed for a bath or to wash our hair, Momma would heat some on the big old kitchen stove. Carrying the hot bucket with a washrag, she'd take it out and pour it directly into the bathtub. Then, she'd add cold water testing the temperature with her elbow until it was just right.

The old cook stove in the kitchen used natural gas, stood on four tall skinny bowed legs, had four burners on the left, and a large double oven on the right.

When the winters would get real cold, Momma would light both the ovens. Leaving the doors open for the warmth; we'd all make pallets and sleep on the kitchen floor. It always seemed a little like camping out to me. I liked it!

Neither my sisters nor I had ever lived more than two blocks from Woodrow Wilson Elementary School and 4th Street Jr. High. (The WPA and the North Little Rock School Board had somehow seen fit to put both of these schools in the same building).

The house just beside ours was the home of Bobbie Belle Priest. A maiden lady, who along with her aging and reclusive Mother had lived there for my entire life. Bobbie Belle would sometimes pay Neecy and me 50 cents each to do little odd jobs like window washing or dusting around the seemingly pristine small white cottage.

Whenever we worked there would always be an extra treat. Sometimes a little slice of buttery pound cake, or a piece of rich chocolate candy from the ever-present "Whitman's sampler."

A younger and almost exact replica of her Mother, Bobbie Belle was always perfectly coifed, painted, cologned and corseted. Even on weekends it seemed that if she had only just stepped out of her Chenille bathrobe and the matching slides, she would've been ready to attend a ball.

Bobbie Belle, like her Mother and their house, smelled of dusting powder, "Evening in Paris" cologne and mothballs. The somewhat dated furniture was all slip covered, or draped in heavy floral chintz. It was also very overstuffed, much like its owners, a pair of perfectly matched pouter pigeons.

The two women seemed rich and very exotic to Neecy and me.

Oh playmate, come out and play with me.
My dolly's got the flu,
Boo hoo Boo hoo, hoo hoo.
Climb up my rain barrel...

The small backyard was separated from ours by four gnarled stunted peach trees, and a wasp infested grape arbor. The woven vines of the arbor led like a secret, hidden path right up to the sloping raggedy door to their cellar. Knowing full well that I wasn't supposed to do it, and usually, before I would even know what I was doing, I'd creep silently through the arbor keeping my eye peeled for wasps, and quietly throw the latch.

Then slowly, still without a sound, I'd gingerly lift the wooden doors with their peeling paint, and making every effort not to be heard, hastily slip inside.

There I'd stand squinting in a ray of dusty sunlight, while waiting for my eyes to become accustomed to the darkness, marveling at almost visible mysterious, dank, dusty wonders standing in arranged disarray before me.

Momma and Bobbie Belle had warned me, on more than one

occasion that the cellar was strictly forbidden territory. But, I was irresistibly drawn to this friendly dungeon, and spent countless hours sifting through wondrous things in their printed boxes, or, plundering down the long plank shelves lined with dusty old bottles or Mason jars, each containing some mysterious things immersed in luminous pastel liquids. Each held an overwhelming enchantment for me.

There were peaches, berries, green tomatoes, cucumbers, and here and there some extraordinary things, which I couldn't identify and which I certainly would never have eaten.

I was willing to risk almost any punishment in my addiction for this puzzling place.

"Sonny Wilson, I'm gonna tell your Momma if you don't get out of that basement right now."

Bobbie Belle's Momma yelled down from her perch at the kitchen window. Flying up the decaying wooden stairs, I'd then hurtle headlong through the grape arbor and the peach trees, to the security of my own backyard. Escaping just in time the wrath of the old woman.

"I'm gonna tell Momma on you."

Neecy was always around, spying on me. Then as if it was her business, she'd run and tell Momma or Sister Jo on me for whatever I'd done.

"You're just an ole tattle tale Neecy."

"I ain't neither, but Momma says that you ain't sposed to go in that cellar."

"I asked!" I lied, goading her on.

"Liar!" The goad had worked.

"I'm gonna tell Momma you called me a liar!"

This usually served to hush her up. Especially since Momma always told us not to call each other liars, or fools.

Diagonally across the street from our house on Second Street, there stood another row of ramshackle old houses. Completely identical except for their degree of deterioration, their fading color, or their occupants, these three little shotgun cottages were totally undistinguished.

The center of these was occupied by John Henry Green, a "slow" young man, along with his Momma and Grandma. He was tall, gawky and strangely handsome, in that way reserved for angels. John Henry, who after being born just like the rest of us, had somehow mysteriously, unexplainably become frozen in time at five years of age. Now, somewhere in his late teems or maybe even his early twenties, John Henry had lived there for as long as I could remember with the two women. His Momma was just a little bit slow too, if you want my opinion.

Cleaning up at the Firestone during the day, occasionally John Henry was allowed to pump gas, or check the oil in the customer's cars. Most often though, he would just be allowed to wash and scrape bug guts from their windshields. Sometimes, when things would get a little slow you'd see John Henry just standing smiling on the curb, waving and smiling at the Traffic as it passed up and down Third Street. Shoot, some of the drivers' would even honk at him as they passed.

After finishing his days work, and after having eaten whatever supper his granny had cooked, you would often catch him as he prowled soundlessly and catlike between the houses, or wandering through the alleys of the neighborhood looking in trash cans or inspecting the neighbors refuse, picking up things and putting them in his pockets like they were important.

Always uninvited, and without so much as a howdy do, he'd join the folks who were attempting to escape the stifling heat of an Arkansas summer on their front porches or in the shady enclaves of their backyards. Walking right up, and plopping down just as pretty as you'd please he'd sort of join the party. Most of the families around Second Street had long since gotten over being put off by John Henry.

The problem was, a body could never tell where John Henry might turn up. If you just rounded a corner, or suddenly glanced up at your window, he might be standing right there just gawking at you.

"Whatcha doin' Sonny?"

It was enough to scare the coon dog shit right out of you.

Sometimes, when he wasn't talking, John Henry looked like he might be all right. You know, almost natural, just like the rest of us. However, if you looked straight into those wandering Periwinkle Blue eyes, you could tell, somehow you could just tell, that John Henry had been allowed to escape from the real world, entering into the safety of his own.

Momma would always say: "John Henry's all right Sonny. I don't think he'd ever hurt a soul...But now, as far as that goes, it's his granny, ole lady Green, that I wouldn't trust as far as I could sling her."

If the truth had been known though, Momma really trusted very few people. Something in the way she had been brought up had made her wary of folks. And, it wasn't just with strangers or outsiders. Momma was even wary of her own family.

I know that blood is thicker than water, but to Momma even that blood was still a little bit runny. To the best of my knowledge she never had any real friends- only acquaintances. Lady friends that Momma might have worked with or women from the neighborhood didn't often drop by our house just to gossip over a cup of coffee or a glass of iced tea.

December's sky was velvety black and crystal clear, with each star twinkling distinctly, distant yet somehow seemingly within our reach. The temperature was hovering just above freezing as the four of us walked back home from Little Rock. No one though, including Momma seemed to mind the cold.

When we left Second Street in late afternoon it was cold yet sunny and bright. It had taken us almost until to dark to get to the State Capital building. This was the night when they lighted the Christmas tree on the Capital lawn. There was a choir and we all sang along with the words printed on the small folded paper that had been handed out by shepherds or wise men. Then there had been a live nativity scene, during which little baby Jesus squalled until the Virgin Mary had embarrassedly changed his diaper. Aunt Maude and Uncle Arthur hadn't gone to Little Rock with us that night. I guess because of our excitement we had barely taken noticed.

The anticipation of the season and the gifts it was supposed to bring was almost too much for Neecy and me. Sister Jo was out of school for the Christmas holidays, and Momma had finally gotten back on her feet from the stroke. And, just in time for the holidays she had found a job working in the bakery of a neighborhood grocery. We all knew that soon Old Santa would be showing up with things for each of us, even though Momma had been trying, unsuccessfully, to caution us not to expect too much.

I was holding tightly to Momma's hand, and Sister Jo was holding Neecy's as we slowly crossed the river on our way home. Our labored breathing was making small clouds in front of our faces, as we trudged up the incline towards the center of the bridge.

I didn't want to let on to Momma and my sisters, but I was a little bit afraid of the height of the bridge and the swirling black waters far below. Other kids in the neighborhood said that there were whirlpools that could suck a person right down if they fell off the bridge. They said a little boy had fallen from the bridge last year, and had never been seen or heard from since.

We had been taking turns quietly singing the Christmas Carols we had heard at the Capital as we walked slowly home. Now, as we reached the center of the bridge Momma's light soprano voice urged us to join her in her favorite carol.

"Away in a manger no crib for a bed,
The little Lord Jesus lay down his sweet head,
The stars in the sky look down where he lay,
The little Lord Jesus asleep on the hay."

Looking down at the water, I was mesmerized by the distorted reflections of the lights from the buildings of Little Rock.

The incandescent Technicolor swirls were being bent and reshaped then quickly reshaped once again by the fast currents of the river as it parted then met itself again around the pylons that supported the bridge. I started the next song.

"You better watch out, you better not cry,
You better not pout, I'm tellin' you why...
Santa Claus is coming to town.

Soon I was joined by my sisters, and then finally by Momma herself as our little voices blended with the mist of our breath floating out over the river.

The house on Second Street had never been wired for electricity, but we really didn't know the difference. Christmas was coming and the small house was fairly sparkling, with or without incandescent lights.

This was the first Christmas we were to spend without our daddy, and the first one Neecy would ever remember. It is still the only Christmas of my entire life where Santa Claus made a personal appearance at our house.

The flickering light from the kerosene lamps was casting a yellow orange glow on the tinsel, and reflecting off the few glass ornaments decorating the small lopsided cedar Christmas tree. Me and Momma had carried the little tree all the way home from the curb market, closely followed by Sister Jo who as always held tightly on Neecy's small hand. Momma had to bargain fiercely for the tree. But finally, after invoking a few demands for Christian charity, and mentioning the plight of the poor widow woman, she was able to get it at her price.

The lamps made a silhouette of the tiny tree on the wall of the small living room, which along with the dancing shadows of Momma and my sisters reached almost to the ceiling. Everything, even the warmth from the red glowing radiants of the gas heater seemed to intensify our excitement as the arrival of Santa Claus approached.

"Ho, Ho, Ho." Rang out somewhere in the darkness!

Hurrying to the windows and hastily rubbing circles so we could see through the frost on the panes, the three of us kids gaped, wide-eyed and speechless as Aunt Maude, with a flashlight in her hand showed old Santa the way to the front door.

Entering through a volley of "Ho, Ho, Ho's" and an almost imperceptible cloud of Sen-Sen, Santa Claus now began working a Christmas miracle. After sitting down in Momma's rocking chair beside the cook-stove in the kitchen, he took the bag from his shoulder, sat it down on the floor, and reaching in, began producing little gifts for each of us, including Momma.

Magically, the modest little house on Second Street had been transfigured into a fairyland of small, sometimes pre-owned, toys, clothes, hard ribbon candy, mesh bags straining under their weight of fruits and nuts, and an abundance of love. Even Momma seemed, if at least just for the time being, that a cloud had been lifted from her shoulders, and as if worry was a long ways off.

The delights of Christmas lasted almost through New Years. It was then that the weather took a very bad turn. Overnight, it had gotten so cold and wet that we had to stay inside, soon succumbing to cabin- fever. It was now nearing the middle of January.

"Hon, I don't think y'all ought to go outside! You'll catch your death of cold."

"Aw Momma, I wanta go play with Billy and Pledger." I whined.

"Now Son you heard me!"

Watching my breath as it frosted the windowpane, and then guiding my fingers through it, I had now begun making intricate patterns in the frosty mist. There was no snow, but as far as the eye could see, everything including the trees, was completely coated with a thin shell of gossamer ice. In places the icicles seemed as if they might touch the ground as trees and shrubs leaned wearily under the weight of their heavy burden.

"Lordee, that hurts."

Momma was standing by the stove making circles with a fork in the big iron skillet. Watching as the mixture of bacon grease and flour slowly began to bubble, and then to brown. An old chipped yellow enamel bowl half full of a mixture of canned milk, water, salt and black pepper sat beside the stove patiently waiting its turn to be added to Momma's lumpy cream gravy.

"Sister Jo, come take out the biscuits, I got to sit down." Momma said, clutching at her side then sinking into Neecy's little rocker that always sat alongside the stove.

"What's wrong, Momma?" Sister Jo asked. Moving smoothly to the stove, and taking the fork from Momma's hand, Sister Jo continued making circles in the quickly browning roux.

"Oh it ain't nothin' hon. I just feel a little peaked."

Expertly grabbing a rag, Sister Jo opened the oven door, removing the golden brown biscuits just in time, all the while never missing a stroke in the bubbling flour. Pouring in the entire bowl of liquid, she continued to stir the hissing steaming mixture as once again it began to bubble, and then quickly thickened into rich cream gravy.

"Oww Sonny, run over and git Missus Evans."

Mrs. Evans was the only person in the neighborhood with a telephone.

"I declare Miz Wilson, if it wuz'nt for bad luck yall wouldn't have any" Miz Evans said as we waited for the ambulance. Sister Jo and Neecy were both crying at the thought of Momma being taken away, but I was more than a little excited by the idea of an ambulance coming to our house. Just wait till I got to tell the other kids.

"Hush Hon, it's gonna be all right." Momma said, taking Neecy's hand and patting it.

After receiving the hurried call Mrs. Evans had made to the excelsior plant, before the ambulance arrived, Uncle Arthur had shown up and taken charge. We all began to wail as the attendants strapped Momma into the gurney and began rolling her out to the waiting ambulance. Neecy began begging to be allowed to go with her.

"Y'all quiet down now, the hospital will take good care of your Momma." Arthur said.

The Doctor said he had gotten to Momma just in the nick of time. If he hadn't seen her when he did, her appendix might have burst and god knows what all. For the two weeks it took for Momma to mend in the free ward at University Hospital, it was necessary for us kids to go live with relatives. Neecy and I moved in with Aunt Maude and Uncle Arthur, while Sister Jo, because of the space, would have to stay with Mattie and Lloyd.

Every afternoon after school Betty would walk the eleven blocks to see us, where she'd straighten up Aunt Maude's house and do the dishes. Then, after supper, she'd walk the two blocks back to Mattie's.

They say: "It never rains unless it pours."

Well, I don't know anything about that, but for a while there it was just like Miz Evans had said. "If it wouldn't a been for hard luck, we wouldn't have had any luck at all." My best present that Christmas had been an almost new, freshly painted bright red, "Western Flyer" wagon. Holding the wagons tongue with both hands, my right knee on the bed, I'd propel myself along with my left foot. As fast as I could push, I'd go racing up and down the sidewalks of Second Street.

It was Saturday morning in early spring, and as she did every Saturday, Momma was hanging clothes on the clothesline while Neecy helped Sister Jo clean the house. Also, as usual, I had been excused from any thing that might be considered women's work. Having just completed another trip around the block, I stopped the wagon on the corner in front of Mrs. Evans. Momma said I had to walk the wagon across the streets. Taking the tongue of my wagon, and after looking both ways, I started across Elm.

I never saw the car. I suppose it was just too far away. Momma heard the crash though, and turned just in time to see my body fly into the air and across the street as the little red wagon disintegrated. I landed in a crumpled heap in the front yard as the car sped away.

I barely remember hearing Momma's scream as she ran over to me, lifting me into her arms just as the blood began gushing from my mouth. As she lifted me, both my shoulders fell limply back from my neck, and moaning, I passed out from the pain. Both my collarbones had been completely shattered.

Luckily, Mrs. Evan's son had seen the entire thing and gotten the license number of the car. When the police arrived at his house to arrest the suspect, he was still drunk. His wife, who had been in the car with him, would later testify in court that he had intentionally run me down.

"We was arguing and he seen the kid starting to cross the street a couple of blocks ahead of us. He turns to me and says, just like it was nothing."

"I'm gonna run over that little bastard."

"Lord yer honner, I didn't believe him at first, but when he started to speed up I commenced hollering and trying to get him to stop! Lord, I sure hope that little kid ain't hurt too bad."

Physically I was healing all right, but the trauma had caused me to be badly frightened of cars and of crossing streets, without my Momma or my big sister by my side.

The University hospital put me in a cast and sent me home providing that I be brought in every week for them to monitor my progress. When Momma wasn't able to take me for my appointments it fell on Aunt Maude to do it. Making each trip an adventure, sometimes she would decide for us to walk over the bridge and catch the streetcar out to the hospital. Other times when she had the money, we might even take a cab.

After my weekly examination and X-rays, sometimes we'd have Nu-Grapes and ham salad sandwiches in the small cafeteria located in the hospital's basement. Other times though, when Aunt Maude had some real shopping to do, we'd eat downtown at the "Pepper Pot," or at "Frankie's" (also a cafeteria). After a lavish dessert, the two of us would slowly poke through the big expensive department stores on Main Street. Not that we were able to buy anything, but it was always nice to pretend.

I was then, and in some ways still, I remain my Momma's boy. I was never an athlete or a participant in sports, but rather a casual spectator. Not always by personal choice, but because Momma would never have allowed me to play a game where I might run the risk of being hurt.

"Now Son, be careful, we ain't got no money for Dr. Burns."

I wasn't unpopular in school. I was something far worse; insignificant, undistinguished, and more often than not just overlooked. I had gotten through my time at Woodrow Wilson Elementary without being noticed, but now I was going to have to settle down and serve my dreaded three-year sentence at 4th Street Junior High School.

Remember when schools were brick, and the wide wooden-floored halls were bordered by rows of metal lockers, each with a small round combination lock? When the whole place smelled of eraser dust, food cooking in the cafeteria, and a little bit of sweat? You know, kinda good and kinda bad at the same time? Well, that was 4th Street Junior High.

One could get to Junior High from Woodrow Wilson elementary school by just walking down a corridor that attached the two.

Those of us who thought we were cool would never have considered walking back into the building where the little kids went. While it was a very short walk, it was a whole world away.

The faculty, in order to keep us separated, made certain there was no overlap of kids either in the cafeteria or on the school grounds. Lunches and recesses were staggered to keep the elementary and Junior High students apart. The only time we shared space with the little kids on the playground was before school in the mornings or in the afternoon when school was over.

In those days everyone without exception was required to go out for PE. This meant physical activity and lots of it. This consisted of running, calisthenics or whatever else the sports crazed coach could think of to torture us. When we had been totally exhausted by the exercise, and when the coach's whistle had completely deafened you, there was the much worse embarrassment of taking a shower in public.

Our family never was...and still is not, a family that talks about our feelings, sex, or our bodies. I was terrified, and more than a little ashamed by the idea of exposing my body to strangers.

Physical Education class was the first time I ever experienced group nakedness, or the awareness of being scrutinized, and where I learned that comparisons were always being made. Most of the time I would attempt to get undressed and into my exercise clothes while being completely wrapped in a towel. Then, when class was finally, blessedly over, I'd slip unnoticed back into my jeans and shirt without taking a shower.

"Wilson, what in the hell do you think you're doing?"

The coach always seemed to catch me, and then to delight in making me an example for the others. At these times, red-faced and ashamed, I'd stand looking down at my feet and mumble.

"Y'all look! Georgy Porgy ain't taking a shower. He's just gonna put his clothes on over his shitty smelling body. He's scared somebody might look at his little dick."

The nervous snickering of the other kids served only to heighten my discomfort. After the public humiliation, and with everyone watching, I'd remove whatever clothing I had been able to get on, wrap myself in a towel and head slowly towards the now almost abandoned showers.

God how I hated PE and that sadistic coach.

It was spring, and a recently divorced, slender horse-faced woman named Virginia, rented the house next door to the Browns and moved in with her three kids. Virginia worked at Kroger's, and Betty, (Neecy and I had stopped calling her sister Jo) had been babysitting Virginia's kids for several weeks when Virginia's younger brother Carl came to Second Street for an extended visit.

Twenty-five years old, Carl still lived with his mother in Batesville. Sometimes he worked as a roustabout in the oil fields down south near El Dorado, Arkansas. Occasionally, when work slowed in the El Dorado fields, Carl would head on up to Oklahoma and work the oil fields there. Most of the time though, he'd just hunt, fish, or lie around his Mother's house drinking and listening to the radio. Sometimes he had even been known to tinker with rundown old cars.

Betty had grown into a sweet and caring young girl, with a pretty if somewhat rounded figure. Her dark hair mirrored the deep brown eyes and the few freckles sprinkled across her button nose. The love she'd always had for Neecy and me was now fully developed into a deep motherly instinct.

Betty had always loved kids. Not just us, but any kids. Because of this, she was a very popular baby-sitter. Popular, not only with the parents, but also with their children. Recently, if still somewhat shyly, she had begun to talk of marriage and having a family of her own.

Momma blamed it all on Virginia! But, regardless of who was to blame, before the middle of Summer Betty was married to Carl, had moved off to Batesville, and was pregnant with their first child. I instantly adored their wonderful little girl, and would for the rest of my life. I believed this precious little red-haired, freckle faced; cherub had been my personal gift from God. Most days after school the baby and I were inseparable. With her in my bicycle basket, and my little mongrel dog Blackie running along at our side; we'd cruise through the neighborhood. Sometimes I'd ride up on the levy and the three of us would just sit and watch the river until almost suppertime.

Blackie had arrived at our doorstep about the same time the baby had been born, and over Momma's objections he had remained. Sometimes, on cold nights when she wasn't watching, I'd even sneak him onto my bed. Sitting all day on the corner just across the street from Woodrow Wilson School the little black dog always waited patiently for me.

Whenever I crossed the street at lunch or when the school day was over, his long tail would wag so fiercely it seemed as if it might throw him to the ground. Even when we were out on the schoolyard at recess, if I looked across the street, there he'd be, just sitting and waiting. In the two years that I had belonged to Blackie, he'd never missed a day on that corner.

After leaving in January for Carl's home in Batesville, Betty and the baby had suddenly returned to us in the spring, saying simply: "Carl and his Mother didn't want us there."

In the early summer of my eleventh year, Momma, bored and weary of her role as the "Widow Wilson," began to seriously explore her options. There had been a false start with a gentlemen friend two years earlier but it had ended rather badly. And, for a while after that she seemed contented for it to be just her and us kids.

Momma had known The McAlister twins, Opal and Oather and their family since way back when she was a very young girl. Like her, they grew up in the foothills of the Ozarks somewhere in North Arkansas. Completely identical, the brothers were red faced, with round hairless heads bobbing above their squat, shapeless bodies.

Oather apparently had taken a real shine to Momma away back, and since he was just recently divorced, he had been trying to rekindle the old flame. For two or three weeks, anytime Momma was off work he'd be hanging around our small rented house on Second Street. Sometimes when he dropped by unexpectedly, it would be around suppertime. Oather was given to slick sharkskin suits in drab grays or navy turning to purple. Usually his outfits came with plaid or printed shirts and wide shiny neckties, and always, almost white socks and scuffed black shoes. He'd look at us kids, and cross his bony legs, exposing a sickening white, blue veined, hairless shiny calf and the elastic straps of his garters. His large red nose had tiny red veins, craterous pores, and looked a little like a roadmap of the moon. He earned his living by selling tractors, and his only transportation was a big old green and yellow flatbed truck with the company's name painted on the doors.

Whenever Oather finally sold a tractor, he delivered it directly to the customer's farm as soon as the loan was approved or the check had cleared, and, before the customer could change their mind.

One Saturday in early spring Oather invited Momma and us to take a ride out towards Hot Springs so he could deliver a tractor. He said that after the delivery we could drive on into Hot Springs, eat lunch at Frankie's cafeteria and then see the sights.

I hadn't been to Hot Springs, and I had heard they had an amazing dancing chicken up there. Now, when I think back, I realize that the poor chicken was made to dance by having heat applied to the metal floor of its small cage, causing it to leap from one foot to the other.

The morning started damp and cold, and rapidly deteriorated into a drizzling, almost freezing rain. But not even the unseasonably cold weather was able to dampen our spirits as we climbed up into the truck. Momma took the middle seat next to Oather, and since I was determined to sit next to the door, Neecy had to squeeze in between Momma and me.

Well, let me tell you, the new owner of the shiny green tractor lived quite a piece off the old Hot Springs highway. Actually, it really was more like a small lane, or a wide path. If Oather hadn't known exactly where he was going, we'd of missed it completely. In some places the slippery red clay ruts were barely wide enough for the truck to pass. We squeaked and groaned along, the trees and bushes lining the sides of the lane scraping against the cab of the truck until it seemed as if there couldn't be a speck of paint left.

Oather's apparent method of negotiating the road was to slam the accelerator down to the floorboard, hang on, and hope for the best.

Winter's hard cold had stripped the dense black tangle completely bare of leaves. Even bare, the jungle on both sides seemed impenetrable, the bony branches slapped angrily against the windshield with each lurch of the truck. Whenever a clearing allowed us to see in front of the truck, there were axle deep ruts already half full of the frigid rainwater. The reddish brown ooze slopped clean up onto the hood of the truck, where the wipers and the branches quickly mixed it into a thick brownish paste. We rocked our way back and forth down the desolate little road, and it seemed at times as if even the truck's big engine wouldn't be able to make it.

Each turn in the road brought another jerking lurch and a new series of snaps and screams as the tractor leapt into the air straining against the chains that restrained it on the truck's wooden bed. Several times the tractor leaped forward, becoming airborne until we thought it might end up in the cab with us. At the last second the screaming chains would grab it again and slam it back down onto the wooden bed.

"Oather honey, is it much further?" Momma asked.

"Naw! I reckon we're about there."

We shot suddenly into a small clearing, where Oather stomped on the brakes and slid the truck around in the front yard of a very small farm.

Well, it wasn't really what you would call a farm; as a matter of fact you might not even call it a camp. The improvements, (at least the ones we could see) were a small, dilapidated house with no porch, a ramshackle chicken house, a doorless two seat outhouse, and an old corral. The only occupant of the corral was a surly looking mule standing with its head in a lean-to and it's ass in the rain.

By the time the scraggly old farmer got out to the truck, the rain had made rivulets down the crown of his hat and created two small streams on each side of the brim, where they met cascading off right in front of his face. The wrinkled old man acknowledged Momma and us with a nod in our direction. It was hard to tell if he was cross eyed, or if the rheumy slits of his eyes were just focusing on the small trickle directly in front of his nose. The faded overalls had obviously been hastily pulled on right over his dirty gray long-johns.

It took Oather and the farmer quite a while to wrestle the ramp out of the truck. Apparently it had been jammed in at an angle the last time it was used. It was only after applying some thick black grease, and several hearty licks from a rusty monkey wrench, that the two men were able to get the ramp back into its track and pulled out of the slot.

Oather sat astride the tractor, and the farmer waved frantic directions from the rear, and finally they were able to get the tractor off the truck and into the lean-to, alongside the chicken house.

By the time they were finished, both men were drenched to the bone, gasping and panting like they had just run a hundred yards.

Through the entire thing, Neecy, Momma and I sat quietly, safe and dry, watching through the rain on the windshield. We had absolutely no intention of spoiling our Sunday clothes before we got to Hot Springs. Momma had hoped for spring by dressing in a light pink dress with a white cinch belt and white medium heeled shoes. Of course her hair and face were impeccable. Neecy also was dressed in pink, but a slightly brighter shade. Momma had braided her auburn hair into two identical pigtails tied with matching satin ribbons. I wore freshly polished saddle oxfords, gray long pants, and an undershirt that showed through the fabric of my pale blue nylon seersucker shirt.

Oather pulled open the driver's door and said: "Y'all come in and sit a while. The farmer and me are gonna dry our clothes by the wood-stove, and then we'll git on over to Hot Springs."

Holding her purse over her head to keep the rain off, Momma hastily threaded her way through the puddles in the grassless, muddy yard. As she hurried towards the house Neecy and I were right on her heels. We darted up the stairs and through the open door, bursting headlong into the front room of the modest little house.

It was really nothing more than a big old unfinished room which served double duty as a living room and bedroom. There was one tattered old chair with a threadbare striped blanket thrown over it. Underneath the blanket you could still make out the faded floral upholstery and the bare spots on the arms and at the corners. There was also an old dresser with a round mirror and a strangely out of place make-up bench in front of the dresser. A chiffarobe standing against one wall completed the décor, except for an old iron bedstead slowly turning to rust, and a chenille covered featherbed mattress.

The whole place was surprisingly fairly neat though. The dominant smells were cigarettes, bacon grease, and chicken-shit.

After dusting at the chair with her lacy white handkerchief, Momma sat gently down, and Neecy and I sat down side by side on the bed slowly sinking into its feathery softness.

We could hear the two men talking in the next room, but we couldn't make out exactly what they were saying. Every now and then there would be a little bit of loud talk, followed by some laughter.

Momma and us sat quietly, and very still, waiting patiently, just as we had while we were in the truck. After what seemed like quite a while Momma got up and gently knocked at the door.

"Oather, how are the clothes?"

Immediately the door opened just a crack. Oather stuck his head around the opening, (we could see the top of his long johns) and said the clothes were still a little damp, and that it shouldn't be but just a little while longer. Then, he pulled the door shut again. Momma got a look on her face, and returned to the chair.

Neecy and me sat there trying not to fidget. (It made Momma mad if you fidgeted.) But the tapping of Neecy's tiny feet against the bedstead got just a little bit louder. It seemed like we had been sitting there for an awful long time and it had gotten a lot quieter in the kitchen when Momma got up and returned to the door. This time she knocked a bit more insistently.

"Oather! Come on now, it's getting late. It's gonna be plumb dark before we get to Hot Springs."

From behind the door we could hear some shuffling. Then, after quite a while longer Oather once again opened the door. This time though, when he finally stuck his head around the door his face and bald head were both bright red, and, he wasn't talking so good.

"It ain gonna be but jus a minit Hon. Y'all jis hol yer horses. I'll be there directly."

"Oather McAlister, you're drunk." Momma said. Then she pushed him out of the way, shoving right past him and into the farmers' kitchen.

There sprawled back against the wall in his dirty long-johns, in the middle of a pile of empty mason jars, laid the old farmer, oblivious to what was happening, and not giving a shit. The old man must have had a still somewhere back in the woods, and the two of them had obviously sampled quite a bit of homebrew. It's a wonder that little kitchen didn't explode as the alcohol fumes from the shine mixed with heat from the stove.

Lord have mercy, but Momma was fit to be tied. The smell of alcohol was almost overpowering as she put her hands on her hips and began to get Oather's sorry ass told.

During her tirade Oather was attempting without much success to get into his still damp clothes.

Then, almost completely dressed, he gave me and Neecy a wink and a smile and sat slowly down onto the floor. Tilting to his side he vainly tried to keep his balance, but finally fell completely over onto the floor where he now lay motionless, passed out.

Then Momma really threw a hissy fit. She didn't hold with drinking, or bad behavior in front of children, and she didn't know how to drive a car, let alone a big old truck!

By dragging and shoving, the three of us were able to get Oather through the house, and across the wet yard. With me and Neecy pulling on his arms, and Momma pushing on his butt, we finally wrestled him up and into the truck. She slammed the passenger door shut behind him, walked around the truck, and slid me and Neecy over to the center then she got in behind the steering wheel. Jerking the door shut behind her, she once again removed her handkerchief from her purse, and spitting on it, began a futile attempt to clean herself up.

She finally gave up on her mud splattered pink dress and resigned herself to wiping what dirt she could off her face. She looked around the truck, tested to see if she could touch the pedals with her feet, and pulled the button marked *Starter*. The huge truck coughed and wheezed its way to life. Every time Momma tried to put the truck into a gear it screamed and leaped forward, until she finally remembered that you had to push the clutch pedal in at the same time.

Torturing the truck into one of its forward gears, and throwing her entire weight at the steering wheel, Momma was barely able to haul it around in the front yard. But, she clipped the chicken-house with the front bumper, only a little tap, but enough to send the reddish brown hens and the old red rooster scattering into the muddy pen in a flying, cackling frenzy. Momma now began to weave the truck in and out of the rutted dirt road and slowly made our way back to the main highway.

The rain and Momma were both unrelenting. The harder it rained, and the further she drove, the madder she became, and the more she got Oather told!

"I don't know why I ever listened to you."

"I always knew you were a drunkard."

"I don't know why I ever thought you was gonna do better."

"I can't believe I've exposed my children to this."

"I could get us all killed."

"You are the sorriest excuse for a man I ever saw."

"I always knew you McAlisters were nothing but trash."

And along we went!

When we finally got back to the blacktop, Momma bumped the big tires up onto the shoulder of the road, and that's where we stayed. Driving as fast as she dared for the next forty miles, all the way to Little Rock, Momma composed her face, and settled into a comfortable speed of about 10 miles per hour. The irate drivers behind us didn't bother Momma at all.

Unable to pass, they honked their horns, waved their fists, and made obscene gestures. Momma just kept on keeping on, and never let up on Oather.

Through all of this he just lay there, snoring in his drunken stupor, oblivious to all around him. Momma's sermon of damnation was falling on very deaf ears. Hours later, when we finally got back to the safety of Second Street, Momma slammed the truck's door with a vengeance, stomped directly into the house without looking back, or so much as a howdy do.

Oather stayed there, passed out in the truck. When we got up the next morning he and the truck were gone, and we never heard from him again.

And I never did get to see that dancing chicken.

For almost a year now Momma had been riding to work at the State Hospital with J.W. The Arkansas State Hospital was way out on Arch Street Pike in Little Rock. It was so far, that it would have taken forever to get there if she would have had to ride the bus.

The wards of the hospital were really just a series of whitewashed dormitories. Each had three floors, and all the windows and doors were behind rusting iron bars. Scattered in a huge semicircle the wards surrounded the eating and recreation halls and exercise fields. The hospital's main building held the reception center and the administrative offices. It was deceptive in as-much as it seemed welcoming and safe. However, if you looked closely you quickly discovered the eight-foot chain-link fence topped by barbed wire keeping the guests in.

All the buildings, including the back half of the reception center were enclosed in this fenced compound. You either left through the front door, or you didn't leave at all.

Topping a hill just behind the Arkansas State Capital building, the Hospital was home to Arkansas's mentally ill, and, sometimes the criminally insane. It housed patients ranging all the way from harmless up to and including the extremely dangerous.

Striking fear into the hearts of most of us children was the occasional escape. Several years before, during a very rare December blizzard, three of the more dangerous inmates had escaped, entered a house, and killed an entire family before they were ultimately captured.

Perhaps there had been some signs of Momma's and J.W.'s budding romance, but us kids hadn't noticed it. More than likely though, it had been concealed from us on purpose. Oh now, don't get me wrong, we had met him all right. A couple of times he had come in and sat in the living room, straight as a rod, his felt hat resting on his lap. He'd sit, quietly and patiently, just waiting for Momma to get ready.

Tall and gangly, with thinning hair, J.W. always looked like he was in desperate need of someplace to put his hands. The rare times when he did speak to us, his voice was soft and gentle. Kinda soothing.

J.W. also seemed to understand how important my place was in the family. He spoke to me like I was almost grown-up. You know, sorta man to man. I reckon if it had been anyone other than my Momma that he was interested in, I would probably have taken to him right off.

"Kids, y'all come in and sit down, I want to tell y'all something!"

Whenever Momma told us to sit down it usually meant there was some sort of problem.

I started planning on how to blame it on Neecy, and eased into the chrome and vinyl chair beside my little sister, staring innocently and intently at Momma's emotionless face. Trying in vain to conceal my apprehension, I began counting the small red squares painted on the ivory top of Momma's old chrome dinette set.

"Y'all know that me and J.W. have been riding to work together for quite a while!" Now I focused on, and began staring intently at the plastic "Aunt Jemima and Uncle Ben" salt and pepper shakers. Not looking up.

"Well, we've decided to get married."

"Aw Momma, I don't like him."

"Oh Son, you don't even know him."

"Yes I do, and I don't like him."

"I think he's real nice."

"He is nice Neecy, and he likes y'all a lot."

"Why'nt you marry someone else? Somebody rich?"

"Now Sonny, you'll see! It'll be all right. I need some help around here, and you kids need a daddy."

"I don't need shit!"

"Sonny Wilson, don't you dare cuss at me. I'll wash your mouth out with Ivory soap. Y'all settle down now, he'll be here in a minute, then we're going over to Little Rock and gettin married. After that we'll come on back and take Y'all out to the Triple A for a hamburger and a root beer float!"

"I think he's very nice Sonny." Said Betty. She had been with us for several weeks now, and there had thankfully been no sign of Carl.

This unexpected and unwanted union, (I didn't want another male around) made it immediately necessary for us to find a larger place to live. Second Street had been just fine for the three of us after Betty Jo had married the year before. But, now with her back, and J.W. and Momma needed their privacy and I was also getting to the point where I could use a little privacy myself.

Carl arrived at the house the next evening just before suppertime, and after Momma and J.W. had gone to work. Neecy was spending the night over at her girlfriend Virgie's house.

Telling Betty how he was sorry and all, begging and pleading for her to take him back, Carl was finally able to get her to go get a cold drink so they could talk privately. Going off in his old Mercury coupe, they left me alone with the baby.

It got dark real late that night. But, after dusk when the darkness finally did come, it slammed down on us like a curtain. One second it was twilight, and the next, before you even noticed, the night had become an impenetrable starless black blanket.

Sometimes, when the weather was real nice, folks would wait for the day to get completely finished before acknowledging the night by turning on their lights. This was that sort of a night.

I was sitting in the kitchen, the baby on my lap, Blackie lying at my feet. The warm kitchen had grown pitch-black, except for the tiny-lighted dial of the radio as we listened to "Inner Sanctum."

Suddenly in the darkness, Blackie stiffened, raising his ears and emitting a low hoarse moan.

Listening without breathing, afraid to move, I was barely able to make out a sliding thump on the front porch, followed by a tiny, almost inaudible cry. Terrified, and very slowly so as not to make a sound, I stood up from the chair covered the baby's mouth with my hand and even more quietly, crept towards the front door.

Cradling the baby in my left arm, with my little dog right beside me, I fumbled, quickly found the latch, and slipped it securely into the little ring. Now, finally safe, I threw the light switch bathing the porch in incandescent light.

There, lying in a crumpled heap on the porch, one shoeless leg twisted awkwardly underneath her body, was "Sister Jo." Slowly she drew the other leg, the white sandal still on her foot, up to her stomach. Both the pale yellow sun-back dress and her dark auburn hair were covered with blood, and her right eye was already swollen shut.

A small stream of blood was beginning to clot where it had trickled from her burst lips. Raising her head my direction she reached out her right hand to me.

Flipping up the latch I hurried out to her as Blackie began to bark, and the baby and I both, began to cry. Setting the baby down on the porch and leaning over, I put my arms around Sister Jo. Pulling up with all my might, until half walking, half dragging, I was able to get her inside the house.

Leaning on me until we got into the bathroom, she quickly turned her back to me so I couldn't see the hurt and said, "Brother, go lock the doors and turn on some light." I heard her lock the bathroom door and start the water in the bathtub as I hurriedly retrieved the baby from the porch and did as she had said.

Sister Jo stayed in the bathroom for an awful long time. After nearly an hour she came out wrapped in towels with her wet yellow dress bundled in her hand. When the dress had been hung up to dry on the backyard clothesline my big sister came back in, sat down beside me, and putting her arm around me gently lay her head on my shoulder.

"Sonny, he don't know what he's doing. It's just that sometimes when he's a little drunk things don't seem right to him."

"But sister Jo, he hit you."

"Shush, I know it Hon, but it don't mean nothin'. Now you promise me you won't tell Momma. OK."

Well, I didn't have to tell Momma anything! Betty's poor bruised face and the bloodstained dress on the clothesline told it all for me.

I'd been in bed when Momma got home, but I could hear the row in the kitchen.

"Now Liza don't carry on so loud, you'll wake up the baby."

"J.W. it ain't right for a man that age to beat a young girl like this."

"Momma, he didn't mean anything."

"Sis, why don't you go on to bed and let me talk to your Momma."?

"He knew she was a kid when he married her, I ought to put the law on him."

The first thing the next morning, over J.W.'s objections, Momma had him drive her downtown to the Square Deal pawnshop where she bought a shiny 22 caliber pistol, and a box of bullets.

All that day and the next, Momma had J.W. drive her to all the beer joints and dives where Carl usually hung out. She said (and I still believe it) that if she had caught him she would have killed his sorry ass. I suppose it's a blessing that she didn't find him, but then again, maybe not.

It would never have occurred to Momma, and she would never have admitted it, but Betty was only doing what she had been taught. In those days, southern women (or girls) would put up with almost any treatment to keep the family together. To turn the other cheek or to look the other way, in an effort to show some misguided gratitude to the breadwinner. Not that Carl was any kind of a breadwinner, but he was the father of my sister's child.

My Daddy had been same type of "Southern Gentleman" as Carl. He beat my mother when he got drunk, or when they fought, which I understand was most of the time. Yet, in my entire life I never heard her speak a single harsh word about my father.

Two days after Betty had been so badly beaten, my little dog Blackie was absent from our meeting place on the corner. Searching through the neighborhood for him, I asked everyone I saw if they'd seen a little black dog? No one had!

In fact, Blackie would never ever be on our corner again. I don't know how many nights, after having once again searched the neighborhood, or pleaded with God to return Blackie to me, I'd finally fall asleep from sorrow, exhaustion and the unbearable emptiness of a broken heart.

Many years later, visiting Betty and the girls in Long Beach, California while on a weekend pass from the Navy, she slipped and told me how Carl, in one of his frequent drunken stupor's admitted one night, how he had drowned my little dog. That dirty rotten bastard.

Momma and J.W. had been searching for several weeks before they finally found a place that was not only acceptable, but also affordable. They'd learned about it from a friend who worked on the ward with J.W. at the hospital. He mentioned to J.W. that there was a three bedroom house out on West Third Street that had just gone up for rent. The small tidy house had been freshly painted, had hardwood floors, and, while the rooms weren't real big, they were neat and clean.

There was also a great big back yard, but the most important feature to me, was that I would finally have my very own bedroom. The promise of this private bedroom substantially eased any anxieties I had about leaving the familiarity of Second Street.

I have never been able to remember the exact time when Eddie and I stopped being just schoolmates and became friends...but I do remember how, and where.

It began in that season we all eventually enter, where too soon the anger and deceit of puberty replace the innocence and wonder of a quickly vanishing childhood. It was somewhere between when I left the sixth grade and the security of elementary school, and entered what was to become the last completely carefree period of my life.

It was a time when we knew no fear, a time when we were

invincible, and when bad things happen only in the movies. It was endless, or so it seemed. All of us were acutely aware that we were growing up, but all the while we felt as if we could not, would not ever grow old. I had never had a friend, at least never a real good friend. And, I had never known anyone who wanted nothing in exchange for spending time and friendship on me.

So far it hadn't been a normal autumn...

Usually, by this late in the year it would already be very cold and mushy with fallen leaves rotting alongside the curbs and in all the gutters. Autumn's chill should by now have created its seasonal cloud of depression, laying it like a shroud over the shoulders of the basin in the Ozarks which contained Arkansas's Capital city, and its small twin on the north side of the river.

Autumn's melancholy usually disappeared during the cold blowing rains of winter, giving way instead to the sweet expectations of Thanksgiving, Christmas, and the treasured two weeks off from school.

In the crisp autumn of 1952 however, Indian summer seemed reluctant to say good-bye, still hanging on, even in October, refusing to relinquish itself to fall. Even at midday, the sun glowed bright orange, casting everyone and everything golden with its unseasonably warm light. And, all day, there had been a gentle northern breeze propelling peach-streaked clouds across the deep blue sky.

Both the clouds and the azure sky would eventually become hidden by the crystal darkness of a clear autumn night, when the magenta and Lemon pinwheels of the setting sun saw us off to bed.

Fall, when the hillsides encircling the Twin Cities went overnight from deep green to gold and ruby, splashed here and there with yellow and lime. When the ground became a dappled technicolor carpet, crunching and crackling under every step. These were the days when walking home from school could take an eternity, which was okay with us because we thought that eternity still lay ahead of us.

Little Rock and North Little Rock share a valley between the foothills of the Ozarks and some undesignated low hills to the southeast. Divided by the Arkansas River winding its way to join the Mississippi, this sheltered valley cuts a deep east west path through the hills. On the west the limestone shoulders of these hills hang out over the river, stopping the cities and ending any idea of further expansion.

The craggy bluffs on the North side of the river are home to Fort Roots Military Hospital. But, on the south side the gentler bluffs held the mansions of doctors, lawyers, politicians and rich merchants. Clinging to the hills like wasps to a hive, these mansions were a source of enchantment and some jealously to the poor kids from both sides of the river.

It seemed as if I had always known who Eddie was. One of those people who is always visible and in the center of things. Seemingly comfortable with being there, Eddie commanded, apparently even welcomed, recognition. Once he had even been on the Junior High football team, actually playing in a game. He'd carried the ball only once, but he did score, lettering that year, (as he would often remind me.). I, of course had never even been to a football game, let alone could or would have been allowed to play in one. I was also painfully aware of who was popular...and who wasn't.

Eddie was!

Eddie and I had been assigned to the same period for Physical Education, and to some other class that had something to do with health and personal hygiene. Both of these classes were taught by the physical education teacher (who was also the football coach).

The second class included some confusing films, discussions of germs, and was the predecessor of sex education. Of course, when it came time for the sex part, (eagerly anticipated by the boys) they taught the girls in one class and the boys in another.

A square shapeless mass of a boy, Eddie had a large round man's face, and a body that simply didn't work. Big thighs and calves supported a flat butt, the beginning of a potbelly, and a head that grew straight out of overly broad shoulders. Even at thirteen Eddie always looked like he needed a shave.

Never going anywhere without his red and gray football jacket, this treasured symbol of acceptance had been embellished with a large "4" for 4th Street Junior High, and the all-important football letter.

The bracing quiet of the autumn afternoon was broken only by the sound of leaves crushing under the feet of my new high topped black tennis shoes, and the sound of someone whistling.

I always got new tennis shoes to start the school year with, and Eddie could always whistle. It was really weird. If Eddie heard a tune just once, from then on, he was able to whistle it, and with perfect pitch. I knew without looking around that he was somewhere behind me.

I had noticed Eddie walking home in the same direction as me on those infrequent afternoons when there was no football practice, or when the popular kids seemed to have nothing exciting to do.

"Hey Wilson...wait up."

I turned around just in time to see him quickly slowing from a trot to a walk. As he fell in beside me I shifted my books from my right hand to my left in an attempt to keep from bumping him. He wore a "Tee" shirt, tight blue jeans straining across his large thighs and his flat butt, and of course, the football jacket. In contrast, my ugly green cloth jacket covered the short sleeved striped shirt, and my still new blue jeans, which were rolled into cuffs at the ankle.

"I saw y'all moving in the other day, but I didn't know at first that it was you!"

"D'you live over by Third street?"

"Yeah."

"Whereabouts?"

"Just a little ways down Pike Avenue."

As we walked along side by side, he began talking to me. You know, really talking. As if he actually knew, (or cared) who I was. He told me about his life, his four brothers, his parents (they were both from Brinkley, Arkansas), and his big play (the only one of his football career).

He acted for all the world, as if we had something in common. He

55

talked to me like he thought it was important to make me understand about his life.

It was also becoming clear to me, that he really was interested in learning about me, and my life. This was very strange. Most people who spoke to me only wanted to tell me about them. They couldn't have cared less about me.

About 8 blocks west of Woodrow Wilson elementary and Fourth Street junior high schools, Third and Fourth streets merge, and from then on are called Broadway. At this juncture, the North Little Rock Ladies Garden Club had developed and now maintained a small wedge of a park. The main feature of this scruffy park was a small and very haphazard Rose-garden, always just a step away from going perpetually to seed.

A couple of blocks further to the west Broadway and the metal culvert paralleling it run under the railroad tracks, dead-ending just two blocks further west at Pike avenue and the café of the same name. Several miles to the North, Pike Avenue becomes the Conway Pike as it heads out of town.

Fifty yards to the left of the cafe Third Street started again, and that's where our new house was located.

By the time we entered the large metal culvert where the sidewalk ran under the railroad tracks, we were beginning to hear the songs being played on the jukebox at the Pike Avenue Café. The unlit culvert always smelled of piss and wine, and its walls were covered with dirty words.

Leaving the stale acrid air of the culvert I was just able to begin to make out the words of the song playing on the jukebox. It was Nat King Cole's new record, one of my favorites.

"A Blossom fell from off a tree
it settled softly on your lips, you turned to me
the gypsies say, and I know why
a falling blossom only touches lips that lie

As it would turn out, Eddie lived right on Pike Avenue just a few houses further down from ours. However, it would be quite some time before I was allowed to know exactly which house was occupied by him, and his family.

When we reached the corner of Third and Pike he hastily mumbled something about our meeting after supper for a Coke or something over at the Café. And, that maybe we could take a walk down to the railroad bridge and hang out, maybe even talk to some hobos. I mumbled back sure, but I wasn't really sure at all. Was I being asked to go somewhere and do something or not? It was unusual for me to be asked to go somewhere with another kid, and I was confused about how this all worked. Most of the time when I wasn't in school, I spent alone. I'd either walk through the woods or sit at home just me and Neecy, and listen to the radio.

I stood at the window, hidden by the lace trimmed cafe curtains watching for him. (To be there first would have seemed too desperate). When he was just barely visible through the kitchen window I flew out the door letting it slam behind me. Trotting over to where he was, I quietly fell into step beside him.

"You got any cigarettes?"

"Naw. d'you?"

"Yeah, I stole a few from my daddy," he said.

I took the somewhat bedraggled Camel he offered, and leaned forward over the flaming Zippo lighter. Trying to look cool, I drew in a deep puff, then, quickly hacked and coughed it back out.

"I bet you ain't never smoked before."

"I have too, my big sister lets me smoke when she's here."

"Got any money?"

"Yeah, I got a quarter."

I had swiped a quarter out of the old blue teapot Momma kept in her china cabinet.

"Let's get a coke and listen to the music."

Cranking the handle until a Dr. Pepper was visible, I put in my quarter, pushed the lever, and then opening the door removed my Dr. Pepper. Reaching over, Eddie took my change from the return slot put in my dime and took out his selection, an RC. Walking into the station he traded my remaining nickel for a bag of peanuts. Any peanuts that didn't go into his RC he then poured directly into his mouth.

We eventually ended up sitting in the damp grass at the back of the filling station, drinking our cold drinks and listening to the songs bought by someone else's quarters. We heard Bill Haley, Laverne Baker, Nat Cole, the new "black screamer" Little Richard," and Eddie Fisher.

"Oh mein papa, to me he was so wonderful,
Oh mein papa to me he was so good"

Eddie knew the words to most of the songs, and with a not unpleasant baritone he'd sing along to the ones he liked most.

"Heart of my heart, I love that melody.
Heart of my heart, brings back a memory.
When we were kids on the corner of the street...

It was the beginning of my journey.

A journey not far in distance or in time, but one of great length through the space of our adolescence.

Eventually, I would find out that Eddie's family was even poorer than mine. His reclusive and overly religious father Bill, worked at the Mill and his wonderful jolly mother Nellie worked at Kroehler's Bakery. All day, every day Nellie stood by a conveyer, where, with a minimum of deft strokes, she'd swirl colored frosting onto each passing cake.

Eddie was the oldest of five boys, identical except for age. Next to him came Bill Jr., then Aubrey, followed by Marion and Bobby. All five of the children were born at curious two year intervals, always in June.

Try as he might to keep me out of his house, I was finally able to get Nellie to invite me in when I dropped by one day knowing that Eddie wasn't home. When Eddie got home from football practice his first reaction on finding me there was to try and find some reason for us to leave. But, Nellie was cooking, and it smelled real good...

As poor as they were, there was always enough to share with me, and not one of them ever seemed to mind. It soon felt, at least to me, as if I had always been a part of their family.

Nellie had an ageless cherubic face, the sort of face, upon which time is impossible to measure. Wizened, but not necessarily wrinkled, neither young, nor old. The gray streaked blonde hair formed a permanent halo around her face, and the shapeless legs were always jammed into worn white crepe-soled shoes. All the women who worked at the bakery were required to wear white nylon hose. Nellie twisted these into knots just above her ample knees. The white of the stockings softened the large deep blue and purple veins lying like gnarled fingers across her tired legs.

Because I didn't judge, and perhaps because I was so thirsty for companionship, and the desire to belong, I quickly became a fixture at Eddie's house. These were wonderful days of acceptance, warmth and joy. Even when Eddie wasn't there, I felt perfectly comfortable with Nellie and the other boys, and seemingly, them with me. No matter what they were doing, I was always welcomed in and made a part of the activities. In truth, I had begun to spend much more time with Eddie's family than with my own.

I had never been exposed to people so open with each other and with outsiders. They laughed often and loud, frequently shouting, or even crying openly whenever there was a reason. This was a family completely different from mine, a family where there was little whispering, but lots of yelling (both good and bad natured).

Now many years later, I understand that what had drawn me into the heart of this simple family was their love for each other and life. Love in its purest, simplest form, unqualified and un-judged, the kind of love that's given freely for the joy of giving, asking nothing in return.

Momma and us would never have talked about our feelings the way Eddie and his folks did. We were never allowed to yell, or even to laugh real loud.

"Y'all hush now, don't be so noisy. What will the neighbors say?"

It was not respectable, or appropriate, or becoming, to make yourself the center of attention. (Someone might ridicule you.) We never saw nakedness (that's nasty), and we never had outsiders in the house. (They might take advantage of you).

The main thing we had, and that Eddie's family didn't, was our shame. It felt as if we carried responsibility for some past sin, or a crime that we didn't commit, but somehow deserved to be punished for.

"I just don't know how I'm gonna hold my head up."

Momma always concerned herself more about the reaction of neighbors and her acquaintances than about the solution to the problem itself.

"Dear lord, I just don't know what the neighbors are gonna think."

Always discouraged from dreaming, and from being dissatisfied with what we had, we had to learn early on to accept things as they were. It's impossible to fail, if you don't dream of change, which by necessity also includes risk.

"Be satisfied and thankful for what you have, and don't think about what you don't have."

Despite all our differences though, here we were, Eddie and I, becoming the best of friends. In the afternoons, I would wait for him or him for me on the front steps at school for the long walk home. In the mornings, I'd wait in front of the Pike Avenue Cafe for him to join me on the walk to school. In the evenings, after having eaten supper, his whistle would signal me to join him at the Cafe or in the field.

When our families finally did get telephones we'd spend endless hours talking to each other, plotting our adventures and painting our dreams.

Directly across the street from Eddie's house the Missouri Pacific Railroad owned a large piece of land. Just an open field really, it was bordered on the north by Broadway. The other boundaries of the field were the railroad embankment (with tracks crossing the river on the Baring Cross Bridge), the Arkansas River, and finally Pike Avenue.

The main features of the huge rectangular lot (six square city blocks), were a tremendous round fuel storage tank with a precarious open metal stairway spiraling up its side, and the abandoned concrete foundation of a building now long forgotten. Six feet above the ground, and about twenty feet square, you could only reach the raised platform by a very steep staircase with a somewhat rickety handrail on only one side.

Eddie would soon become bored with the service station, and begin strolling towards the field. In what was to become a sort of ritual, I'd fall in alongside him. During the first few years of our friendship Eddie would always lead, and I would always follow.

Later this would change...

Climbing the stairs up to the foundation, we'd lay flat on our backs, the sounds of Nat King Cole or Frankie Laine barely audible from the cafe. The chill of autumn numbing our legs through our jeans, there we'd lay, smoking stolen Camels, staring at the black velvet sky and its clutter of rhinestone stars.

We talked very little on these nights. Mostly Eddie asked me questions, the kind that I hated, the ones that required me to answer.

That first night in the field he asked:

"Is that little girl your sister?"

"Yeah."

"Where's your Momma and Daddy work?"

"At the state hospital, and he ain't my daddy."

"He ain't? Where's your daddy?"

"Dead!"

"Dead?"

As autumn gave way to winter, then spring to summer, the MoPac field became the site of our dreams, our plans, and our fantasies, (not always sexual). Sometimes without speaking, we'd just watch the slow interplay of stars, and breathe in the unnatural heat of the Arkansas summer.

"I sing as good as ol' Eddie Fisher! I wonder how you get to be a singer?"

"Shoot Eddie, you're already a singer. You just ain't famous."

"You know what I mean, Wilson."

"Yeah."

"Let's go down under the bridge and talk to the bums."

"My Momma said I ain't supposed to go down there." I lied to cover my fear.

"You're just chicken shit."

"I ain't either. let's go."

I guess I really was sort of chicken shit. Not really afraid of the bums themselves, but afraid that we might run into my Uncle Leroy down under the bridge with the rest of the bums. The hobos always seemed real eager to talk to us. It seemed to me, like they really enjoyed telling us their stories. They'd talk about sex, travel, drinking, or whatever bad fortune had brought them to their sorry state.

Eventually, Eddie and I were joined in the field, and in our friendship, by Hal and Joe. A year younger than Eddie and me, Hal lived two blocks further down Pike Avenue. A ruddy muscular kid, Hal and I were almost exactly the same height. His curly brown hair, his deep set brown eyes and olive complexion made him seem almost foreign, kinda like he was Italian or something.

Joe on the other hand, was very tall and slender, with eyes like shiny black coals. His blue black hair was so dark as to seem almost unnatural next to his pale perfect alabaster skin. The envy of many girls, Joe's rosy cheeks and full lips made him look almost feminine.

Joe's family lived diagonally across the block from the back of my house, directly behind the Cafe. He had quit school the year before, and at sixteen seemed much more mature than the rest of us. As far as we were concerned, Joe was a man.

Joe's little brother Mike tagged along behind him wherever he went. Like a faithful dog, Mike was always just a few steps behind Joe and us as we looked for mischief, or searched for our next adventure.

Joe's younger sister Jewel was my age, sharing two classes with Eddie, and one with me. Attractive in a funny sort of way, Jewel's eyes were just a little too large, her neck just a little too long. She kept her dark hair cropped into a poodle cut, and always wore pink. Sometimes just lipstick or fingernail polish, she always had some pink somewhere.

Hal lived with his divorced mother, his beautiful younger sister Celinda and a devoted, rambunctious, three-legged mutt, named

Coco. Coco lost his left front leg as a pup, when Hal's mother had accidentally backed over him with her car. Reddish brown with black tipped ears and snout, Coco seemingly was unaware of his disability. And, kinda like Mike, he was always just a few steps behind us.

Considering himself our protector, Coco ran along ahead of us, until some perceived danger, a covey of startled quail, a rabbit, or some other threat rose up from a tree or bush. Then, growling and tossing his head, he'd do a three legged skip, run into the scrub, bark ferociously, and, after a few minutes, come hopping back to his place alongside Hal.

Every day, from early morning, sometimes right on through until dusk, we'd spend the eternal hours of summer hiking in the woods of Fort Roots, climbing the craggy limestone cliffs of Big Rock, crawling through the dark confined mystery of Wolf Cave, or running stark naked across the scorching sandbar for a swim in the tepid waters of the Arkansas River.

The sandbar stretched west from the railroad bridge, right up to the cliffs of Fort Root. Covered over by water in the winter, the sandy peninsula was our summer beach, the deserts of Egypt, or the uncharted surface of some distant planet. It was also the summer home of snakes, turtles, bobwhites, and most of the time to five or more tanned, often naked young boys. It seemed so removed from the rest of the world that sometimes we forget where we were. From the last day of school it served up daily fantasies, until the rains of winter once again caused it to disappear. When we were on the sandbar, the mansions on the cliffs of Little Rock and the hospital on the bluff ceased to exist.

Invincible, and invisible to all around us, or so we imagined, our awareness was completely confined to whatever fantasy there was to be spun, or whatever opportunity there was for an adventure.

Each spring when the sandbar reappeared, the hearty river willows would begin another small new forest of saplings on the east end of the sandbar. Unaware of their sure death at the hands of the rising waters coming each fall, these hardy trees sprung up from the sand. With trunks no bigger than a boy's finger and with tops only slightly taller than our heads they formed a doomed miniature maze providing relief from the heat, and the doldrums.

Like these saplings, our days on the sandbar were also numbered. Not, by the rising river, but by the changing seasons of our lives.

In what was to become our final year on the sandbar (the summer between eighth and ninth grade) we erected what we thought would be a permanent structure. We wove the pliable and living branches of the willows into a small hut, to be used it as a place to escape the sun, eat whatever we had, and sometimes, even to sleep through the heat of the afternoon.

We didn't know, and couldn't possibly have imagined that we would never return to the sandbar, at least, not all of us together.

The river held a wealth of curiosities, each competing for our attention. One of the most fascinating was Vestal Plant Nurseries, which occupied many acres of land on the north side of the river. The well-tended fields of domesticated flowers and the huge meandering greenhouses of frosted glass kaleidescoped right up to the edge of the bluffs of Fort Roots. In the winter these heated conservatories became welcome relief from the cold and wet as we wandered our way to or from the adventures being offered by the surrounding woods and cliffs.

Not far away, standing like a scarecrow in a seasonal field of brilliant yellow lilies, stood the abandoned Vestal Mansion. Two huge oak trees, their ancient branches now growing parallel to the ground, framed the once majestic old house. The trees completely obscured the third floor, the widows-walk and the two chimneys standing sentinel at each end of the slate roof.

Slowly being demolished from neglect, left alone to fight the elements, the once magnificent old Ante Bellum building was now a home for vermin, wandering hobos, and occasionally some eager young boys and a three legged brown dog.

Fascinated by the old house, and the spell its charm produced, we made up stories about its past (always splendid), and its future (even more splendid). We soon knew each plank or tile intimately, having explored every square inch many times. Once, standing quietly on the bottom of the attic trusses, Joe and I had watched through a hole in the tongue and groove ceiling where the planks had rotted away as far below a hobo completely unaware of being watched, peed, then took several long drinks before discarding his now empty muscatel bottle still wrapped in it's brown paper bag.

It was one of those nights when dusk came early, but dark would not come until very late. Sitting between the monstrous oaks around a small fire Joe had built, we eagerly waited to eat potatoes that had carelessly been thrown into the flames. The fire never produced enough heat to cook the potatoes completely through, but the skins were always blackened long before they were done. But, with an abundance of salt and the ever present hunger, the half cooked potatoes weren't too bad.

The cinders from the rapidly dwindling fire wound their way up and through the huge bare branches of the oak trees, where the chill of the autumn evening rapidly smothered them.

"I'm gonna git my Momma to buy this place, and fix it up."

"You ain't gonna do shit, Eddie."

"We could fix it up and make a clubhouse."

"How you gonna fix anything?"

"Y'all can't do nothin to nobody else's house." Joe's level headedness usually brought us back to reality.

"Momma says they kilt a nigger here!" said Mike.

"Who kilt a nigger?"

"The Ku Klux!"

"Why'd they kill him?"

"Cause he raped a white girl and killed her, left her up on that flat part of the roof."

The last rays of sun glinted off the pale green glass of the greenhouses, then died as crickets and other night creatures began their nightly serenade to the darkness. Fireflies were beginning their nightly journey up the riverbank in search of their evening feast of pollen, nectar, or love.

Suddenly Eddie's hand shot out as he grabbed one of the hapless bugs. Quickly tearing its head away from its phosphorescent tail, he smeared the glowing remains onto his forehead.

"I'm a lightning bug."

"You're a dickhead." I replied.

In the suddenly pitch-black night, Mike still refused to leave it alone.

"Yeah, they say he cut her up in brick bats up on the roof."

"Shut-up Mike, you're makin' that shit up."

"I ain't neither. They dragged him all over town from the bumper of a police car, then they cut his dick off, stuffed it in his mouth and burned him up under that big old tree."

"I'm gonna cut your dick off if you don't hush."

"Momma says the little girl comes back sometimes."

We all felt it more than heard it. Was it the wind, or something else? Well, whatever it was, it made the hair on the back of my neck stand straight up. Coco bristled, muttering under his breath as again we all heard the second low mournful moan.

For a second we were frozen: soundless and motionless.

Then our fear led first to frightened flight, then pandemonium.

Scattering into the darkness we ran, stumbling, falling and getting up to run, only to stumble again. Dropping the half eaten, almost raw potatoes, we made our frantic escape from the demons in the darkness.

Amazingly enough, Eddie, as big as he was, was the first to reach the safety of streetlights at the corner, but only by just a very few steps. The embarrassment of shared fear also caught up with us at the corner. So far as I know, none of us ever heard or spoke another word about the "Nigger" or the girl.

Sometimes at night we'd gather at Joe's house for games, usually cards, and most often Hearts. It was here that I first tried drinking beer. It was also here where I also learned that people inflicting physical and emotional pain on the ones they're supposed to love was not unique to my family.

Joe and Jewel's mother Marie (who looked a lot like the movie star Jean Tierney) worked at the clock factory, and their crippled father sold ladies shoes at Rephan's. On paydays he'd usually come home drunk, dragging his platform-shoed foot, looking for and usually finding a reason to fight with and then to beat his wife.

The only one who could stop these attacks was Joe.

"Now goddammit it, Daddy, you got to stop this shit."

"Boy, don't you cuss at your daddy."

"I'll do more than cuss if you don't git on to bed and leave Momma alone."

"I'll take my belt off."

"Daddy, just go on to bed...Please."

Marie would quietly move out of the room while Joe calmed his daddy. Then, after washing the hurt off her face, she'd sometimes come out and join us on the porch. Sitting on the top step with her feet on the next, Marie would lean over, quietly lay her head on her knees, and wrapping her arms around her legs allow her dark hair to cascade across, then cover her face.

We had spent the entire day since early morning on or in the river. Sometimes swimming, sometimes just lying on the bank. Mike had gone to pee, while the rest of us lay, naked, unashamedly sprawled as if we had been cast onto the mud by some giant hand. The summer heat was so strong you could see it rising in great shimmering sheets from the banks. The only relief was the occasional thermal breeze that felt like someone was fanning heated air over your body.

Every now and then a fast moving tugboat after having deposited its sand filled barge up-river announced its passage with the sound of its powerful engines, or by allowing its horn to whistle at our nakedness.

Scrambling into the water, paddling as fast as we could into the tugboat's wake, we'd lie, just floating on the water, letting the rhythmic waves toss us up and down like fishing corks. The ever diminishing ripples were cool and sweet like the aftertaste you get from eating orange sherbet, lasting long past the noise of the boats engines.

We had swum across the river at Big Rock that day, leaving our clothes heaped in piles on the sandbar.

Finding our perfect spot on the south bank we had then defiantly paraded our nakedness ashore. The rivers bank at this point sloped steeply upwards until it was twenty feet or more above the water.

Ancient woods on both sides of the river now hid us, and the bank from all except the most observant voyeur, or those who worked on the river.

Away to the west, in the bend of the river dominating the view rose Pinnacle Mountain. Because of its flat top we always imagined (even wished) that Pinnacle was a dormant volcano, lying there just waiting for a small earthquake or one of our adventures, to awaken, then, to violently erupt, spewing forth lava, smoke, flame, causing death and destruction.

We lay, coasting halfway between sleep and wakefulness when suddenly we were startled by a frantic movement from the bank to the right and high above us. Before we could get turned around Mike hurtled out of the tree, off a vine, and shot way out into the river making a huge splash as he entered the water feet first. Quietly he had climbed a big old vine-wrapped river elm where he had discovered an exciting new toy.

Hal was the first to follow Mike into the tree, but soon we all were playing Tarzan. All, that is, except Eddie.

Because of his size Eddie was having a difficult time climbing up the vine covered trunk, and of course the rest of us were making no effort to help.

"Fuck Y'all" he hollered, shooting a fat finger up into the branches in our general direction.

Angry and desperate, Eddie grabbed another, lower hanging vine, and started his lumbering run towards the edge of the bank. As his feet left the ground he swung at a right angle to the river. Then, just as he cleared the edge of the embankment, there was a sound like a shotgun, *BLAM!* And the vine gave way.

Hurtling through the air ass first, legs up, arms flaying, Eddie's big ponderous butt plowed into the bank like a huge pink bulldozer. Sliding across the bank ass first, forcing mud up his crack, he finally slid to a halt just at the water's edge.

There was an ominous quiet, and then suddenly an unholy scream. Later, even Eddie would laugh and say it sounded like "a dying calf bellowing in a hail storm."

Even if he had been killed we would all still have been hysterical. Laughing and clutching at the tree we slowly made our way down from its branches.

When we finally got down to the bank where he lay half in and half out of the water, he had rolled over onto his stomach to give his butt some relief. The cheeks of his ass were deep red and it looked like someone had hand packed the entire crack full of slimy river mud and bits of grass.

Joe said "I betcha he'll shit dirt for a month" and once again we all fell into hysterical spasms of laughter. If there was ever anything redder than Eddies butt, it would have had to be his face. For the rest of the summer, any time he went to the toilet, we heard a whole new series of whines and moans.

The last month of summer was when I took my first job. Old Man William's lived next door to Joe and Jewel and had a big old open bed truck over which he had rigged up a tarpaulin. He'd drive that old truck through the poorest black neighborhoods selling picked over fruits and vegetables. He had hurt his back loading turnips and needed someone to help. That someone was me. It paid fifty cents an hour, which seemed like a fortune to all of us. We had to start out real early. Momma'd get me up at 6, and the first stop would be the curb market. In most places these are called farmers markets, but in North Little Rock it always was and still is called the curb market.

Mr. William's bought whatever was cheap, which usually meant that whatever it was, it was also almost spoiled. Picking off the worst parts, we'd spray the days merchandise with a borrowed hose, and head for Congo Corners, the white folks' name for the worst part of the black neighborhoods.

Old Man William's offered credit on the produce, and because money never changed hands until Saturday mornings, he was able to charge an arm and a leg for his sorry merchandise.

Working didn't leave much time for me to fart around with Eddie and the others, but it did give me something I had never had before...spending money! At least in my own mind I had now become a big deal. I was the one who always had money to go the picture show at the Juroy, or the Rialto. I also got to treat for cokes and candy at the drug store or a hamburger at the Pike Avenue Cafe.

Labor Day came and school started before any of us could get ready. The warmth of summer extending into September caused the school room windows to be open, and the river breezes continually beckoned us back to the sandbar or the field. I continued to work for Mr. Williams on Saturdays as summer slowly gave way to fall. As the days became cooler we lay out later and later on the concrete embankment across from Eddie's house. We had learned to sneak a little bourbon from Joe's daddy, and Eddie always had some cigarettes stolen from Bill or Nellie. Sipping the foul tasting bourbon and warm coke added to our other new sensation, approaching adulthood.

Sometimes, when we'd get a little hungry, and under the cover of darkness, we'd sidle up to old man Williams truck. There, we'd help ourselves to bananas, grapes, watermelons or whatever was the freshest. A couple of times we were a little noisy and Mr. Williams almost caught us. But since he always turned on the kitchen light and started hollering, we were able to get away before he recognized us.

"Guess what, I'm gittin' hair on my dick."

"So what Eddie, I got plenty of hair on mine."

The four of us were lying on our backs on top of the big oil tank when Joe responded to Eddie's announcement.

"Wilson's dick is as bald as my daddy's head."

"Screw you, Eddie." Raising up slightly I was able to strike a gentle glancing blow at his crotch.

"You better look out asshole, I'll whip your ass."

"You better pack a lunch pigfucker, it'll take a while to whip my ass."

"I'm hungry, Y'all hungry?"

"What's new? You're always hungry!"

"Lets go git us some watermelon."

It was pitch black when Joe dropped onto his stomach, and followed by the rest of us began inching his way along. Slowly, and quietly we slithered across the open field toward Mr. Williams's truck. The last fifty yards or so became pure torture due to the burrs and the piss ants.

"I hate this shit. What if they's snakes?"

"Shut the fuck up, Eddie. This was your idea."

Arriving at the truck, and in the protection of darkness, we rose silently to get a better look. I grabbed a few bunches of Concord grapes, while Joe and Hal took apples and an orange or two. Eddie had already filled both hands, his pockets and his mouth, but was determined to get just a couple more bananas. Extending his arm and hand he reached further into the truck until there was a sudden snap *"CH-CLUNK".* Eddie sucked in his breath then made a little whistling whiny sound. "Oh shit...Oh piss...Oh fuck me."

Eddie's banana filled hand had been ensnared. Snapped and locked tight in a small animal trap. Afraid of making any noise for fear of getting caught, the rest of us ran, loping and giggling back across the yard, throwing ourselves once again into the shelter of the weeded field.

"Oh man, what the fuck are we gonna do?"

"You gotta git him out, Joe.(We always looked to Joe to fix things.) Old man Williams will put the law on us if he catches us."

"We gotta go back and git him loose."

An almost inaudible "eeeuuuwww" came from the direction of the truck and once again we began snickering.

Joe crawled back towards the truck, back to Eddie, standing only when he had reached his side. Hal and I sat crouched, watching from the weeds.

As the light in the Williams kitchen came on Joe put one leg up against the side of the truck, grabbed the trap with both hands, and pulled with all his strength.

Whang! The nails holding the trap to the truck's wooden sides gave way and Eddie was free.

Joe and Eddie flew back across the field towards us strewing fruit and dragging the trap as old man Williams, dressed only in his long johns burst onto the porch cussing and waving a stick.

Finally back in the safety of the fields by the stairs leading up to the tank Hal found a small stick and with the leverage we were able to pry the small animal trap off Eddie's slightly mangled hand. Holding his huge hand out to the dim light from the Cafe he moaned as he assessed the damage. It was already beginning to swell, but Thank God, it was only minimal!

Looking down in the dim light, Joe noticed the widening dampness at Eddie's crotch.

"I'll be goddamned, this big sissy pissed his self"

"Yeah, well it hurt, motherfucker."

Laughing hysterically we began wolfing down what was left of the fruit. There were a few tiny holes and some scratches on Eddie's hand, but his badly bruised pride would take a while longer to heal.

The very next day Mr. Williams fired me.

My first job, and the first time I was fired paled in the face of something else new. A marvelous thing happened just as I was entering the ninth grade. I began to grow some pubic hair. Just a sparse blond frizz at first, but I couldn't have been more proud.

Maybe I was playing catch up, but now at least I was in the game. Finally I could take my shower with out being totally embarrassed, and maybe with even a little bit of pride.

Eddie and I had been assigned to the same music class, and somehow our being able to stand or sit beside each other made me begin to feel more secure than I ever had. These were the days of "What it was, was football," and "Grandma's Lye Soap."

"Do you remember Grandma's lye soap?
Good for everything in the home.
And the secret was in the scrubbing,
It wouldn't suds, it couldn't foam."

Mrs. Trailer, the music teacher; announced that she was planning a minstrel show, (yep, the kind with blackface), and that auditions would be held for an interlocutor, and six end-men. It was to be a grand variety show, and would take place in the 4th Street auditorium the week of Halloween. Everyone in the music class was very excited, but none more than Eddie. We were both certain that he would be chosen as the interlocutor or at the very least an end-man.

We rehearsed every day to make certain that Eddie would be chosen. Reading his lines and doing the skits with him, I was constantly amazed at how natural and easy it all seemed for Eddie.

Eddie's black dialect was completely natural.

Well, it was maybe a little bit like Amos and Andy, but it was natural for North Little Rock in the fifties. It was great fun playing straight man for Eddie. But, as time went on, and our practices intensified, I discovered that I too loved the idea of "putting on" as Momma called it. It is a love that has never left me.

The day of tryouts came, and Mrs. Trailer arranged all the eager candidates in a semi circle around the piano in the music room. As each pair was called on to read their lines, each of us made a silent judgment and then our choices. The first to go was Ralph Hicks, who at 16 was the oldest kid in school. Ralph had been held back twice. The following summer Ralph quit school, and joined the navy. He was swept overboard and drowned his very first week at sea.

Everyone knew Ralph would be chosen. One of the funniest guys in school he had a reputation as a prankster, and even the teachers loved him. Claude Deloach (who could laugh on cue in falsetto and was Ralph's partner) was also sure to be chosen. The auditions seemed to fly by, and before we knew it, it was time for Eddie and me.

We began somewhat slowly, and Eddie's Black accent (perhaps a little too exaggerated) began to cause some small ripples of laughs. But, by the time we got to the end of our selection everyone in the room was hysterical with laughter, including the music teacher and the other faculty members.

After everyone had finished, Mrs. Trailer thanked us all and said that the names of the cast would be posted on the door of the music class after school.

The suspense was so thick you could taste it. Moving like slugs through the rest of our classes that afternoon, we mumbled when called upon, thinking of just one thing…

Racing from PE class to the music room, I began to fear that Eddie might be disappointed! What if someone else had been better? What if he hadn't gotten the part he so badly wanted?

We both nearly fell over in shock when after shoving our way through the small crowd we saw that not only was Eddie to play an end-man in the minstrel show, so was I. It was absolutely the high point of my young life.

During rehearsals I began to feel that I was no longer just one of many, not just Eddie's partner. But now, I too, had begun to be noticed by some of the other kids. Now the acceptance I had never had, and had never admitted I wanted, was coming to me. No longer did I sit by myself at lunch, or stand alone at recess, watching the groups of kids. My face had now become attached to a name, and the other kids knew it.

I had gone overnight from being ignored to:

"Hey Wilson, how's it hanging?"

or "Y'all wanna git a coke at the Pike on the way home ?"

The costumes were blue jeans with stripes of red grosgrain ribbon sewn on the legs by our mothers, (quite a task for Momma), and white shirts with red bowties and matching suspenders. As I stood admiring myself in Momma's vanity mirror I thought I looked splendid. When we added the black face, bright red cheeks and ivory lips I knew I was bound to be a hit.

The big night finally came.

We were all rushing around backstage doing those little last minute preparations, fussing with our costumes or makeup, and listening as the audience began to enter, and most were suffering with a very severe case of stage fright. I thought my heart was going to jump out of my throat.

Mrs. Trailer tried to be reassuring, but I knew now that it had been a big mistake for me to take the part. I was going to be booed or hissed right off the stage, and it was just what I deserved. Who did I think I was anyway?

But, as I relaxed into the part a new sensation began pushing the stage fright aside. The audience was responding, laughing at all the right places, and applauding each of us in turn. It became obvious early on, even to me, that I was the favorite. It seemed completely natural to play to the audience and hold for laughs. As I rose to the situation, so did the others.

If I exaggerated even the slightest bit, Eddie or one of the others would take my cue. Rising to the slightest provocation we had all begun, shamelessly playing to the audience for laughs.

A walk became a strut, a nod became a bow, and the more we did the more the audience responded.

I could see Momma and J.W. in the audience and even they both seemed to be having a good time.

As each of us took our bows, the applause was tremendous for Eddie, but it was even more so for me. At first I didn't know what they were doing as they stood, and it was only later that Mrs. Trailer told me it was a "standing ovation." Lots of people came backstage, but I already knew that Momma and J.W. would have headed on home.

On our walk home after the show there was a light drizzling rain but we didn't mind. Our small group became fewer and fewer at each intersection until finally it was only Eddie and me.

"Wilson, I got to hand it to you, you were pretty damn good up there."

"You were pretty good yourself."

Still in our costumes, including the blackface, we strolled down Third Street as the rain intensified. Imperceptible at First, then a little bit harder, then harder still, until before we knew it the rain was blowing in horizontal sheets across Third Street. There was no place to hide, and it was much too far to the culvert for us to run.

So we continued to stroll.

In just the few blocks to the little park, the streets and sidewalks had become flooded, and cars were beginning to stall out in the rising water. At the merger of Third and Fourth there were at least a half dozen cars stopped and in serious danger of being covered by water. Eddie took off his shoes, rolled up his striped pants and began pushing cars to higher ground. Without an instant's hesitation I joined him.

We were quite a sight in the drenched costumes, with the black makeup leaving circles around our eyes, and turning our collars gray. As we went about our labors other drivers began splashing out of their cars and into the effort. In just a very short time the road was clear, and as the grateful drivers honked their thanks we continued our walk home.

This was the first time I can remember doing something completely spontaneous. Normally I would have weighed the consequences and then, probably have chosen not to participate. Or, things would have been over long before I would have been able to decide what to do. And of course, I would have heard it when I got home.

"Son, you have to be careful what you do. Folks might think the wrong thing or you might get hurt."

"How could you get into that water, you could take your death of cold, and look at your clothes, you've ruined them."

Throwing our drenched clothes into heaping piles on the floor we both fell across the bed, already asleep. As usual I was spending the night at Eddie's house. Staying over was now more comfortable for both of us than going home.

It had taken Eddie almost until Christmas to decide it was okay for me to be inside his house. Poorly furnished, and incredibly messy, it was also constantly filled with laughter and the smell of something good to eat (if you didn't think about where it was cooked). How I envied him.

With the five boys, the full time job, and taking the bus to and from the bakery, Nellie didn't have a lot of time. Because I didn't judge Eddie or his family, they accepted me easily as a new addition to their family.

Eddie was the only kid with his own room. His parents had their room of course, but the other boys all shared the last of the three small bedrooms. From these frequent nights at Eddie's house I was able to learn another reason he didn't want overnight guests. He frequently wet the bed.

Horribly ashamed of this, he never discussed it with me or anyone else that I knew of. Every night though, at bedtime, when we'd go in to go to sleep, his bed would be freshly changed, and the mattress turned and dried as if nothing had happened the night before.

We ate Chili-Mac at Eddie's house, and after banana Jell-O we headed for the field. We sat on top of the fuel tank, and it was here that Eddie first began to hint that there was some sort of trouble with Nellie and Bill. It was just a feeling you got, nothing that he actually said or anything you could see, just a feeling. He'd talk about them like they weren't his parents, saying things like:

"If they don't like each other, why do they have to stay married?"

Several weeks later I found out that Nellie had a boyfriend. At our age I was not sure of what that meant, or why, but it was a source of great sadness for Eddie. Eddie and Nellie had become distant somehow, as if they were no longer relatives but just polite strangers. They'd always been very affectionate with lots of hugging and touching. That had disappeared seemingly overnight and been replaced with a reserved indifference.

Eddie was now very cold to Nellie. Most of the time, you couldn't tell if she noticed or not, unless you looked into her eyes.

Either the others weren't aware of the change, or they just didn't care. Eddies daddy sure didn't act like he had noticed anything...

Mike was the first to break the news: We had climbed over the locked gate at the bottom of the long skinny staircase and made our way gingerly to the top of the huge fuel tank. It was always a little frightening on the small metal steps watching the ground recede and feeling the wind as we approached the slightly conical top. Of course none of us ever let on that we were a little frightened by the climb. Lying in a circle with our heads almost touching we searched the skies and felt the first fingers of the north winds that would soon drive autumn away, leaving the wet cold of early winter to have its way with North Little Rock.

"Y'all guess what! Daddy signed up for Joe to go to the Navy."

"You lying pigfucker." Eddie laughed. "Joe ain't old enough!"

"He is too," Mike whined.

"Momma's real pissed off at my Daddy. She says he only wanted to get rid of Joe so's he can raise all the hell he wants when Joe ain't here."

Joe had gone to the grocery store with Marie and Jewel that night, but you can bet that we were waiting on their porch when he got home. He seemed excited by the prospect of being flown to California and going on a ship. Though Marie said very little, we could tell that she was saddened by the thought of losing her son, her protector and her friend.

Before we knew it, it was time for Joe to go. It seemed like he was gone almost as soon as we heard that he was leaving. His daddy was too drunk, but the rest of us walked with him and his family over the bridge to the bus station. Marie talked the entire way to the station, like she thought that if she stopped long enough to start crying she might never stop.

Mike and Jewel, like the rest of us said very little, but our faces said plenty. It was not manly to hug, so Eddie, Hal and I each in turn shook his hand. Jewel and Mike hugged him, and Marie gave him a quick kiss, mumbling something about being careful and being sure to write...He stepped onto the bus, the driver shut the door and Joe was gone!

The void left by Joe was more surprising to me perhaps than it was to anyone else. I had always thought that I was closer to Hal and Eddie than I was to Joe. Didn't I spend almost every night with Eddie? Didn't Hal and I sometimes go to the picture show, walk to school or eat lunch together, or sometimes go out on the sandbar, just the two of us?

Now it was different, I didn't cry, but I felt like it...Joe had been our leader, our protector. Joe was always the one that made sense, the one who figured it out, the one that knew what everything meant or how something should be done.

At first we looked at pictures of him in boot camp, or when he went on his first ship. We were eager to hear where he was and what he was doing. Then, it became easier and easier to forget...

Eddie hadn't mentioned anything about his Momma and the boyfriend for a long time now, but it was apparent that the situation between them had changed. They were more like they used to be. There was now laughter where silence had prevailed.

There was now hugging where there had been no contact. And,

best of all Eddie was the old Eddie. Things weren't completely back to normal yet, but it sure looked like they were headed in that direction.

Football season was on us before I noticed that Eddie had not gone out for the team. Or at least that's what he said...

Nellie let slip one night about their not being able to pay for a uniform or any of the other costs associated with being a "Member of the team." Eddie simply dismissed it by saying; "Shit, it ain't nothin but a fuckin' old game nohow."

In those days the only place to play sports was at the high school stadium and that's where we had gone to watch 4th Street get the shit kicked out of them by Conway Jr. High. This was a wonderful experience for me. The autumn night had grown cold with nightfall, and it was great sitting by Eddie on the wooden bench watching the mist from your breath, cussing and hollering along with the other kids, occasionally raising a finger to the opposing team.

Maybe best of all though was the other kids passing and saying:

"Hey Eddie."

"Hey Wilson."

"What y'all up to?"

I was exhilarated simply by just being noticed, by being singled out without being scorned, and by just being allowed into Eddie's world.

After the game we walked with a group of other kids the 18 blocks from 22nd Street down Main Street. There was a dance going on that night as we passed the Boys Club and started our climb up the three block long viaduct that spanned the MoPac railroad tracks. We could see the high school kids embracing in the dim light and rocking slowly back and forth to Gail Storm:

"Come down, come down from your ivory tower,

Let love come into your heart

It's cold so cold in your ivory tower,

Don't keep us so far apart."

The Saturday morning was cold and remarkably thick with fog. Recently, we had discovered that on such a morning you could climb the cliffs of Fort Roots and from that vantage point look down on fog clouds as they hugged the land. Awaking early to pee I discovered the dense fog and after a bit of coaxing was able to get Eddie up so we could go share this phenomenon.

We heard the report of the rifle and the whine of the bullet tracing its jet-stream through the impenetrable fog before slamming into the already dead black walnut tree. Eddie and I had just left the warmth of the orchid greenhouse and were making our way across the Vestal property towards the small hills that rose up to Fort Root.

"Watch out mother fucker, there's people over here." Eddie hollered.

"Who's that?"

"Me and Wilson, who's there?"

"It's me, Winston Price," as he came walking out of the fog the barrel of his 22 rifle thrown over his shoulder.

I'd never liked Price. Once in third grade he'd made fun of my worn clothes. Sometimes too, he'd bully kids who were smaller than he was or those he had his bluff in with. There weren't many victims lately however, since he seemed to have stopped growing at just a little over five feet.

I was now taller than Price, and it pleased the shit right out of me. I'd stand up real close to him whenever I could and let him know that I wouldn't put up with none of his crap.

"You oughta be careful in this fog, you might hurt somebody!"

"They ain't nobody out here this early. Hey, Wilson."

"Hi Price." as I strolled over by his side.

"What're you huntin'."

"Nuthin', I just like to shoot. Wanna take a shot Wilson?"

"Sure." I answered his dare.

"Whatcha gonna shoot?"

"See that little white rock over yonder by the old tree? I'm gonna shoot that."

"I bet you cain't hit it. That's a long ways off."

"I bet I do." I raised the rifle to my shoulder, sighted down the barrel squinting, took aim and fired.

"*Ka thunk*" and the small rock was blown to bits.

"Wow, I bet you'd be a sharpshooter in the army."

"He'd be a sharp shit." said Eddie.

"Fuck you, I bet I'd be a sharpshooter too. If I was old enough, them Korean's'd have to watch their yellow asses."

"I'm glad I ain't old enough. I ain't interested in getting shot at."

"You wanna shoot somethin Eddie, cause I'm almost outta bullets?"

"Naw Price, I gotta take a pee and I wanna smoke a cigarette." as he unzipped his pants.

"If I was in the army, I'd get out!"

"Price, once they got you they'd keep your pitiful ass till the war's over!"

"No they don't, Wilson, you can get out if you get shot."

"Shoot, I'd rather stay in than get killed by some dumb ass Korean."

"All you gotta do is shoot yourself in the foot."

"You're crazy Price."

He took aim at his left foot with the empty rifle and pulled the trigger.

"*Ka-pow*" the bullet he had forgotten in the chamber slammed through his shoe into his foot, pinning the sole of his shoe to the ground.

Price screamed and Eddie stopped peeing in midstream.

"Ohhhhhh, I'm shot."

"Mother fucker! What're we gonna do Wilson?" Eddie asked hurriedly zipping up his pants.

"Get outta the Army I guess." And I began to laugh.

"What're you laughing at you crazy pigfucker ? He's shot."

"Owww, euuuwwwww. Git me a doctor!"

"Come on Wilson, help me," Eddie took Price by the left arm, and put it around his right shoulder.

Taking Price's other side, I intertwined my arms with Eddie's making a packsaddle. Price sat on our arms his arms around our shoulders and we began carrying him towards the office at Vestals, a good half mile away.

I just couldn't help myself. The more Price moaned and cried the more I giggled, until finally Eddie, too, began to snicker. It was all we could do to keep from dropping him on his stupid ass as we stumbled and laughed our way towards help.

Price stayed pissed off at me for the longest time.

"Carolee's invited me to a birthday party for Anita Stockard." Eddie said. I didn't answer, fearing what I knew was to follow.

We were on our way home from the picture show. We had sneaked in at the Rialto and watched the last half of "The Last Time I Saw Paris" with Elizabeth Taylor and Van Johnson. It was okay till she died, then it was kinda mushy so we left and started home.

"You can come, too, if you want to."

"I ain't goin to no fuckin' dance just so you can play stink-finger with Carolee's big pussy!"

"You jerk," he said striking a glancing blow off my left shoulder.

"It ain't no date, it's just a party with some kids and some dancing."

I didn't say anything for a while and slowly Eddie began to sing, Quietly at first, then louder...

"Earth angel, Earth angel will you be mine?
My darling dear, love you all the time.
I'm just a fool...a fool in love with you. "

As I slowly joined in at the chorus, I thought maybe a party and a little dancing didn't seem so bad after all, long as it wasn't no date. I could feel myself and my unknown partner gliding across the floor, just like Marge and Gower Champion. All of a sudden I realized that we would have to glide, since neither one of us had any idea how to dance.

We finished "Earth Angel" and Eddie slipped quickly into the new Lavern Baker tune.

Tweedley Tweedley Tweedley Dee,
I'm as happy as can be...

Well Jiminy Cricket, Jiminy Jack,
You make my heart go clickety clack.
Tweedley Tweedley Tweedley Dee.
Tweedley Dee, Tweedley Dot,
Gimme gimme gimme gimme all the love you got
HUMPTY UMP BUMP BUMP

The crowd had dwindled by the time we reached Fourth Street where we turned right and started towards the Pike. Most of our conversation to this point had dealt with the unfairness of sports, and how great it was gonna be to get to High School the next year. And, how good it would be to get to go to the dances at the Boys Club at 13th and Main Street.

By the time we reached the wedge of the Rose garden and the railroad bridge, the mood had changed. Eddie hadn't said a thing for several blocks and I was trudging along, not understanding the silence or knowing how to break it.

When the sounds and the smells of the Cafe reached us, Eddie began to walk a little slower, then slower still, until finally he stopped completely as we entered the culvert under the overpass.

I was several paces ahead before I realized he wasn't beside me. As I turned and walked back towards him he said:

"She wants us to come to the Cafe and meet the mother fucker,"

"Who?"

"Momma and That bastard!"

"What bastard?"

"That sonofabitch she's been going out with."

Neither of us said a word as we walked slowly towards the Cafe. It felt like we were on our way to something ghastly, an execution maybe. But, it was still a little thrilling to think that soon we would be able see this guy we had only speculated about. Finally to be able to attach a face to the nameless flame.

I don't know what I expected, but he was ordinary...just a regular sort of guy. Nellie said his now forgotten name and then told him ours.

"This here's my oldest boy Eddie."

"And, this is his little friend George."

He slowly withdrew his offered hand when neither Eddie nor I took it. They ordered us burgers and Cokes, the burgers came, we ate them quickly, and then the ordeal was over. Nellie said a whispered goodnight to the man, and the three of us stood, leaving the stranger alone at the Cafe. The night had cooled quickly and we could see our breath as we headed down Pike Avenue towards home.

"How was the game?" she asked.

SILENCE

"Okay" I mumbled.

"Who won?"

"Conway."

What was the score?"

I didn't remember.

At the corner of Third I turned towards my house mumbling something like:

"See ya tomorrow."

SILENCE

I had planned on staying at Eddie's, but something had changed my mind for me.

The next morning when we met on the corner for the walk to school Eddie was changed, more like his old self. Walking to school we discussed regular things like always. Apparently there had been a settlement after I left them, but I was never told what it was.

We never discussed that night again, or the man or what happened after they left me, but from that point on life at their house seemingly had been restored to normal.

What I guessed to be part of the resolution appeared beside Eddie's bed a few days later. It was one of those new 45 RPM record players, an RCA model with no top, a flat front covering the speaker, and a round beige thing that allowed the new smaller 45 RPM records to fit on the turntable.

This was between the end of the brittle 78 RPMs and the still unknown to us 33 RPMs with hi-fi sound. Every time we got seventy-nine cents we bought a new record.

Jewel had also been invited to Carolee's party, and she had reluctantly agreed to teach Eddie and me how to dance. Most days from suppertime until bedtime we'd carry Eddie's record player over to her house and practice on the linoleum floor.

"Start with your left foot"...

"One two three...and."

"One two three...and."

"One two three...and."

This lasted until way after dark or unless her daddy came home on a rampage.

Sometimes we'd take a break from the dancing and play cards. Hearts became almost as much of an obsession as dancing or bullshitting. Having never played cards at home, I was astounded to discover that people actually counted cards or developed strategies. I learned that you had to think in some card games, and that luck was not the only way to win a game.

When Hearts or some other card game didn't get our attention it was "the Mickey Mouse Club" or fantasizing about Annette and getting to go to Anaheim. Disneyland was completely unimaginable to us. A whole amusement park, dedicated just to movie characters...wow!

"Who's the leader of the club
that's made for you and me?
M—I—C—K—E—Y. M-O-U-S-E.

Each of us knew all the words and the names of the kids that sang them every weekday afternoon. Bobby's dancing or Cubby's cuteness became addictive to us, and we never missed a show.

More and more it became obvious to Jewel, Mike and me that as far as the dancing went, I was actually getting pretty good. Poor Eddie, however, was just wasting his time. He didn't have a bit of rhythm or the slightest clue. You could tell by his attitude though that he thought he was really catching on. The day of Carolee's party arrived way before we were ready.

I had been able to pout my way into getting Momma to buy me a pair of pink suede shoes.

"Yes, they can too be school shoes."

"But Son, they're pink."

"I know it Momma, all the kids are wearing them."

"You know we can't afford to buy you new shoes every time you turn around."

"Oh Momma, I promise I won't ask for nothing else, not even for Christmas."

Along with the shoes, I had been able to whine her into buying me a long-sleeved pink shirt with a black collar.

Eddie hadn't been as fortunate however, so we had spray painted his raggedy old shoes metallic silver with "Nestlé's Streaks and Tips for Hair" from the cosmetic counter at the drug store. There was a little bit of paint left in the can, so rather than let it go to waste we used it on our flattops. The directions said it would shampoo right out...We were sure it was going to be okay!

The silver hair and the matching shoes made walking to Carolee's house a little bit like walking in a parade. As we passed folks they'd look over their shoulders, and others would holler for their families to come out onto the porch for a better look.

"Pansy Jean, come see what's coming down the road."

"Don't look back, Junior, it ain't polite."

But the worst of all was:

"Look like some goddam idiot California faggots if you ask me."

Thank you, Jesus, for the arrival of darkness!

The party was a great success and so were we, despite our partners' silver shoulders, and the cloud of silver snow that followed us both everywhere. The "Streaks and Tips" had become our enemy. The only thing that would remove it was contact with any fabric, sheets, pillowcases, blankets, shirt-collars, or girl's party dresses.

Oh yeah, Anita took a big shine to my dancing. Carolee was only slightly bigger than Eddie, and she sort of aimed and pushed him around her living room floor.

But, if it looked and sounded like dancing...well, I guess it was dancing.

Jewel had shown up with a real date, surprising all of us, but especially me. I always thought we were real close, and that she would have told me if she was gonna have a date. I'd have told her if I was gonna have a date!

He was Jackie Minor, a senior, who was considered by some to be the best looking boy in school. Jackie was also a really terrific dancer. Now we knew where Jewel had learned the steps she'd been teaching Eddie and me.

There was quite a crowd at the party. It looked like Carolee had invited about half the kids in school, and some that we didn't even know, (probably Catholics. They had their own schools).

Her Momma and some other ladies had done lots of cooking so there was plenty to eat. They'd also made some kind of fruit punch that was continually bubbling up white mist from the dry ice they had dumped into it. It was very exotic!

The decorations were kinda Christ-massy, with Santa Clauses, holly and an imitation reindeer with a glittered red nose. There was even a small sprig of mistletoe hanging between the living room and dining room.

That damn Anita kept trying to maneuver me under that mistletoe. Whenever I felt her trying to dance and shove me that direction, I'd just dance and shove her big butt back towards the living room.

"George, honey, you are sure funny."

"Don't be callin' me honey!"

Even though it was cold outside, the small house was very warm, and couples kept drifting out to the small brick patio to cool off. On one trip (I made Eddie go with me to keep me safe from Anita's old blubbery lips). I saw Jewel and Jackie on the platform swing, and they were kissing, right out where everyone could see.

It was in early spring that "Sister Jo" left Carl for the final time, and returned to North Little Rock. For the three years they had been married she had been badly abused, both physically and mentally. True to her upbringing however, she had repeatedly tried, sometimes with all her might to make the marriage work. Betty now had a second child, and one almost blind eye from Carl's relentless beatings. Finally, beginning to fear for her life and the safety of the children, she found the strength to end the marriage.

Anyhow, that spring, Betty (finally and thankfully divorced) took me out in J.W.'s old 1950 stick-shift Ford coupe, and with Neecy and the two babies in the back seat started the arduous task of teaching me how to drive. We went to the best place in the world for Drivers Ed, a city with no people, no buildings, and almost no cars.

Camp Robinson was an old abandoned army encampment on the far northern border of Pulaski County. During WW II the army had kept some German POW's at the camp. All that now remained was perfectly laid out city blocks with no buildings, striped by the occasional hedgerow or some long forgotten flower gardens long since gone to seed.

Kudzu and blackberry had won the battle for some of the streets, but there was still adequate blacktop to serve our needs. The Camp also had become a haven for occasional drinkers or romantics, if empty beer and wine bottles or spent rubbers on the streets were any indication.

On the way to the Camp it was necessary to pass the huge red brick Catholic orphanage, which made all us little Protestant kids shiver. We had heard how the nuns killed and ate little unwanted babies, burying their bones in the walls. We also knew that they worshipped statues and devils.

Except for one small mishap, a near miss with a cow that blundered onto the road, my impromptu drivers Ed went fairly well. I got the hang of steering and pressing the accelerator, but at first I couldn't figure out how you worked the damn clutch, brake and gas pedals at the same time, and all with just two feet.

In those days a driver's license in Arkansas was just a simple hand written receipt. There was no written test, but just a short trip around the block with a courageous policeman. Then you filled out an application, paid your three bucks and you were officially a driver. Sister Jo's friend Juanita was married to a policeman, Monte Montgomery. Monte luckily issued driver's licenses. It was a good thing, too. I was still only barely able to manage that two feet thing.

Driving in those days was more than just a rite of passage. It was a step towards popularity, freedom, maturity, and it was fun! Nothing could have been more invigorating than flying along at 35 miles an hour, your arm resting on the door, the small vent window blowing wind and an occasional small insect into your face.

Always hoping for some less fortunate walking acquaintances to see you as you sped past! You could gain their attention by a friendly tap on the horn and a little wave. Not too big, nor too enthusiastic. The age of "Cool" was approaching.

It was Wednesday afternoon in early spring, the first of Momma and J.W. two days off.

He and Momma had been out almost all day paying bills, and on the way home they had stopped by Kroger's where they bought the weeks groceries. Momma spent the remainder of the afternoon in the kitchen cooking supper. Today it was one of my favorites: fried okra, fresh sliced tomatoes, fried pork chops and fried potatoes. All covered with greasy cream gravy.

We usually ate in silence except for the occasional question from Momma and the mumbled answer from me or Janice. This night it seemed more...uh...I don't know...interesting.

Momma had been smiling more than usual, and J.W. had been talking. A lot! He even volunteered that after supper he thought maybe we should take a little drive out to the Triple A Root Beer Stand for a float. (What the hell was going on?)

I almost inhaled my supper, wanting to hurry up for the promised drive, and a root beer float. It seemed like the rest of them were just fartin' around. Momma would cut a bite of pork chop, and before she'd even put it in her mouth she'd ask one of us a question or tell us something about work.

J.W. was talking about the weather. Even Betty was telling about getting a job, or looking for someone to take care of the babies.

Why didn't they just hush? We could talk about that shit on the way to get my root beer.

Finally, after what seemed like a lifetime, they finished and we piled into the car.

Sister Jo, Neecy and the babies got in the back, and Momma took her place in the front next to J.W. She always sat by folding her legs onto the seat, turning slightly towards him and resting her left arm on the seat behind his head.

Hooray! This meant I got to ride shotgun.

Well, the Triple A was in Levy, way out on Pike Avenue, right before the big old Church of God. He passed it like he didn't even know where it was. I elbowed Momma, "What's going on? We just passed the Triple A." Then Momma said;

"We have another surprise for yawl."

"I know I'd go from rags to riches
If you would only say you care,
And though my pockets may be empty,
I know I'd be a millionaire"

As we continued out the road towards that damn orphanage I began to fidget, recalling all the shit I had always put everybody through. Maybe they were going to drop me off there. I was blessedly saved when J.W. made a left turn onto 50th. Street. Less than half a block down the road he slowed the car, turned left across a small concrete pipe recently covered with fresh dirt, pulling the Ford to rest beside a long front porch attached to a small, freshly painted white frame house.

"What do Y'all think?" he asked.

"About what?" I asked.

"Are we still gettin root beer?" Neecy whined.

Betty sat silent for a moment and then asked, "Are we moving?"

Momma laughed a little and then said, "That's what happens when you buy a house."

"Did y'all really buy this house?" Betty asked.

"Shore did...Let's go on inside." said J.W. producing a key from his pocket and in we went. It wasn't new, but it was big and clean, and it had lots of windows.

Best of all though, was that there were bedrooms for Momma and J.W., for me, for Neecy, and even one for Betty and the babies.

The porch had a gray painted plank floor and its roof was supported by six square green posts. Stretching across the entire front of the house, there was even a porch swing hanging from chains. Unbelievable!

It was too fantastic—my own room, our very own house. Neither Momma nor J.W. had ever owned a house, and the rest of us had never even considered it. Our relatives and ancestors on both sides had always been tenants or sharecroppers.

I was busting to get home to Third and run over and brag to Eddie and them about our change of fortune and new status as homeowners. It seemed as if we inhaled the root beer floats, and before I knew it we were back at Third Street.

As J.W. applied the brakes my butt flew off the seat and shot out the door. "Son you don't stay out late now!" Momma hollered.

"OK." I mumbled without a backward glance.

Flying the two blocks to Eddie's house, and hurtling through the front door (I had long since stopped knocking) I realized there was no one home. Then I remembered—Dammit, it was Wednesday and they were all gone to prayer meeting.

The next best thing I guessed would be getting to tell Jewel and Mike. Jewel took my hand and said:

"I'm so proud for y'all George, but does this mean we won't be able to be friends anymore?" I hadn't even thought of that.

"Naw, it don't mean nothin'. I'll come everyday."

"I sure hope so. Since Joe's been gone, I'd sure hate to lose you, too!" she said putting her arm around me.

Suddenly, despite my excitement, the move to Levy seemed like somewhat less of a good idea. It was a long ways off, and it was way too far to walk everyday. When we started to high school next fall it would be a lot closer to Levy than back to Third Street.

How could I be in two places at one time? I had to be near my friends, but my family would be in Levy. When Jewel's daddy got home from work, drunk as usual, I left for the field. As if announcing the end of winter, knee deep clover had covered the field like a hazy purple cloud. Climbing the stairs, I lay down on the concrete foundation, watching as the dark slipped quietly over the railroad tracks.

I must have dozed, because the sound of their voices awakened me. I heard them long before I could see them. Nellie, Eddie and the boys had gotten off the bus and were making their way home through darkness so total that the only beacons were stars or an occasional living room lamp.

Creeping slowly down the stairs I lay on my belly in the clover, crawling soundlessly in their direction. Getting closer I could tell that the conversation was tense, and that Eddie was not happy. He was hanging back from Nellie, letting the younger boys take his usual place beside her.

"Ain't there anyplace else we can go?" he asked her.

"I been looking, honey, and they just ain't anything we can afford..."

"If I get a job, can we not go?"

I leaped up and out of the clover, launching myself at Eddie, screaming as I ran. Nellie hollered and the younger boys hurtled towards their house. Eddie hit me across a shoulder. "You shitass!"

"Guess what? Momma and J.W. bought us a house up in Levy!"

"That's real nice George." Nellie said.

Eddie said nothing. It was as if I had never joined them. Nellie asked questions about the house, when we'd be moving and all, but Eddie didn't say a word. When I tried to involve him in my excitement he only grunted, turning away from me. For the first time in our relationship, I felt like Eddie would have preferred for me not be around. His attitude was so chilly that I finally turned and headed back towards my house saying, "See ya."

We began the move to Levy almost immediately. Momma and J.W. promised that as soon as I could drive they would let me use the car a couple of times a week to visit my friends or for us to go to the Skyline Drive In. The excitement was unbearable, and soon, the memory of that night and the anguished conversation between Nellie and Eddie was forgotten.

The few times that I did think of it, I put it down as something to do with Nellie's boyfriend.

Now, however, the meaning was about to become clear. They were moving too, to Silver City Courts. We didn't know about public housing in those days, but we did know about housing projects. That's where people went when they couldn't go anyplace else. We also knew about Silver City Courts. Having learned about the courts from our parents, we thought it was the last stop before the poor house. We also knew it was admitting, publicly, that you were poor. While almost everyone was poor, no one ever admitted it.

We ate the same foods, and wore the same clothes didn't we? And, almost all of our daddies had used cars. That is, if they had cars in the first place.

There must have been more than fifty buildings in the Courts. Yellow brick two story rectangles each was divided into eight apartments. Each apartment had two stairs up to the front porch, covered by a poured concrete protrusion. The small porches however offered little shelter from the rain.

There always seemed to be a pall hanging over the courts. Perhaps it was caused by the sameness. But, more than likely it was because everyone there admitted to themselves that they had given up, that their dreams were to be denied, and that the Courts were a public admission that they had succumbed to a life of abject poverty.

True to his word, J.W. finished my driving lessons. And, after a trip to see Monte Montgomery, I was cautiously allowed to begin driving. Usually, I'd go to Eddie's first, then after picking him up, we'd go over to Jewel's and Mike's. Several times Jewel's Momma would take a ride with us out to the Triple A or up on Fort Roots where we'd park on top of the cliffs and watch the sun set over the river and Pinnacle Mountain. Other times, we'd go to the Skyline.

The Skyline Drive In had been gouged and blasted out of a solid limestone bluff sitting high above Levy and the Conway Pike. It is still the only drive in theater I have ever heard of that had balconies. Yes...balconies.

The entrance to the Skyline was really heady stuff for a novice driver. The entrance was just a short drive to the ticket booth right off Conway Pike, where, after paying, you steered your car sharply to the left, climbing steeply (and suddenly) to the top row. From there you could look down into the valley, seeing the screen and the concession stand. It was on this upper level where couples going steady or married folks parked.

The top row also afforded an excellent panoramic view of Levy and Highway 5 as it made its way north, first to Conway and from there to parts unknown.

From the top balcony the road serpentines its way down, each hairpin turn becoming a slightly lower balcony until finally the curves stopped and the conventional slope of a regular drive-in presented itself. It was here that families, and carloads of friends, many hidden in trunks until leaving the ticket booth, watched the evening feature.

A small playground directly in front of the movie screen allowed impassioned couples parked on the top balcony to get rid of the kids. When the kids tired of the teeter totter and the merry go round, they could have a seat in the rows of theater seats lined up in front of the concession stand.

We had just left the Courts and were on our way to Levy. Whenever he could, Eddie now maneuvered his way into spending the night at my house, or at the very least staying away until the anonymity of darkness hid him as he returned home to the hated apartment.

"Do you think she puts out?" Eddie asked...

"Who?"...

"Carolee!"

"Huh?" I said, "Everybody says she does."

"I shore would like to git me some...Let's take her and Anita to the Skyline this Friday."

"I ain't goin'" on no date, with that fuckin' fat-ass Anita."

Of course we picked them up at dusk on Friday!

Eddie had stolen a pack of Camels from his daddy, and we had bribed a railroad bum to buy us two bottles of muscatel wine. Eddie and Carolee in the backseat (of course) had pawed at each other through the entire movie (John Wayne in The High and Mighty).

"Goddammit it, Eddie, I don't want to go to Camp Robinson."

We were at the concession stand peeing. Carolee had to go pee for about the fiftieth time so all four of us had made our way down from the balcony, again.

"Aw, come on. I know she's gonna let me have some tonight."

94

When we got back to the balcony Anita attempted to ooch over beside me once or twice, but each time I shoved her back, complaining of the heat and saying "Y'all hush now. I'm trying to listen."

Both girls seemed to welcome the idea of a little drive after the movie, and neither one had seemed even the teeniest bit surprised when we started down the long dark road leading to the Camp. It seemed a little, at least to me, as if Eddie and I were the ones who were being set up.

We were sitting with the windows down in the pitch black bowels of the camp. After we had found the perfect spot (selected by Carolee, of course), she and Eddie started wallowing around in the back seat, making J.W.'s old car rock and groan. I kept to my side of the car. That fat heifer Anita was gonna have to jump the gear shift to get to me.

"Whatsa matter, Georgy Porgy ? Don't you like me?"

I didn't answer.

"Now Georgy honey, I know the cat ain't got your tongue."

"Eddie, you move your hand right now." Carolee whispered from the back seat.

The heat was stifling and the wine was hot, but we were still trying to drink it.

After some more pawing Carolee said:

"I'm about to fall clean out from this heat! Ain't yawl hot?"

"I'm bout to melt." said Anita.

There's nothing hotter than a late summer night in Arkansas. You can just sit or lie stark still, without moving a muscle, and feel the sweat pouring buckets into your drawers. I knew it had to be gushing between Anita's fat titties.

"They ain't a sign of a breeze." Carolee complained again.

"George sweetie, drive a little and let us have a little breeze."

Obediently, I pulled the starter and the old Ford ground, coughed a little, then chugged to life. Weaving back and forth on the asphalt I made my way between the empty blocks of the Camp. Left at this corner, right at the next, then left again or whatever. I left the lights off so we would be undetected by other cars parked in the Camp.

"Go a little faster Georgy, I still ain't getting no breeze."

I pressed the accelerator a little harder…Carolee really did know how to piss me off!

"Stop the car" she screamed suddenly.

I hit the brake, stopping right in the middle of the road.

"What do you want now? goddam it!"

"Me and Anita want to ride on the hood, don't we Anita? And don't you cuss at me George Wilson."

Eddie got out, helping Carolee, Pushing her up onto the right fender (what a gentleman!) He still hadn't had any, and he was already pussy whipped.

Anita got out and hauled her own big ass onto the left fender.

I wasn't moving!…

Eddie replaced Anita beside me in the front seat, and I pulled on the headlights. The old Ford slowly began to move as I eased the accelerator down.

"Did you get any?"

"Hell naw, did you?"

"I didn't want any off that fat sow."

"George honey, drive a little faster. We still ain't cooling off."

I accelerated a bit more.

"She's a pain in the butt Eddie."

"Faster Georgy!"

I pressed down on the gas a little more.

"I know it, I ain't never takin' her nowhere else."

"Well, I sure as hell ain't taking Anita either."

"Won't this old thang go any faster, y'all?"

I stomped down on the accelerator as hard as I could.

The old Ford seemed to stand up on its back wheels as if it was frightened, then it leaped forward. Anita fell back, rolled over on her belly, grabbing the windshield wipers with both her chubby little hands. Carolee in the meantime was attempting to get some sort of a hold on the hood ornament.

"What the fuck are you doin'?" Eddie asked.

"I'm coolin' their fat asses off!"

"Not so fast" was lost in the wind as Carolee's crinoline skirt blew back across her face exposing a pink garter belt and more than ample milky white thighs.

When Anita rolled onto her stomach her straight skirt had filled with air creating an impromptu wind sock. Her already ponderous ass now looked even larger than usual.

"Goddamn you, George Wilson." Anita mouthed through the windshield.

"Help!" Carolee screamed. "Please slow down."

Sitting beside me, Eddie was bent double, convulsed with laughter.

"You crazy sonofabitch, you gonna get them killed."

Unconcerned, I made every effort to press the accelerator right through the floorboard.

"Stop this fucking car you little idiot!" Carolee demanded.

As ordered, and with all my might I jerked my foot off the accelerator and stomped it onto the brake. The Ford jerked a little, the tires screamed, and as we entered the slide, Anita suddenly became airborne, feet first.

Making a futile effort to keep her feet under her big ass, Carolee hit the blacktop running. Her fat little feet were churning the pavement so fast it looked as if her legs were making complete circles. As her butt finally outran her legs, she spun around, flying off the low shoulder of the road, propelled, big titties first into a huge, voracious blackberry bush.

Anita didn't fare quite as well as Carolee. Hitting the pavement belly first she bounced and bumped along for 20 or 30 feet. Then finally rolling over onto her butt she skidded to a complete stop. All the while, never leaving the road.

The blackberry bush grabbed hold of Carolee's hair and one of her falsies and was obviously determined to keep them both. After much struggling and pulling we were able to get it to relinquish most of her hair, but the falsie was forever lost. Also gone forever was the ass of Anita's skirt. It and most of her right eyebrow had been shaved off when she slid across the pavement.

The girls couldn't stop moaning and crying, and each new cry threw Eddie and me further into hysterical laughter. This was definitely my last outing with Carolee and Anita.

What with Carolee's cussing and Anita's pissing and moaning, the drive from Camp Robinson seemed very long, and more than a little tense.

After we dropped Carolee and Anita off at Carolee's house, we were now on our way to spend the night at Silver City Courts.

"Oh…man I'm drunk," Eddie groaned spraying vomit out the window.

He had finished the rest of the warm wine, and we were both now paying the price.

"Oh shit, don't throw up on J.W.s car."

Parking at the public lot at the Courts we stumbled and staggered our way through the maze of yellow brick dormitories to the one that held Eddie's family. Stumbling, and groaning, Eddie vomited almost every step of the way.

"SHHHHH goddammit it, your Momma will hear us." I pleaded.

"Ohhhhhhhhhhhhh fuck me!"…he groaned and fell…

"Shhhhh you dumb fuck!"

Helping him up, he leaned his entire bulk on me. Barely able to stand under the weight

I struggled, dragging him towards his apartment. Turning a corner our legs became entangled and unable to keep my balance I fell with him on top of me. Pushing with both arms and my knee I was able to roll him off and dragged him once again to his feet. As we entered the apartment he belched loudly, and covering his mouth and holding the vomit in, he ran up the stairs to the bathroom.

I could hear him heaving from the bathroom as I tumbled into the extra bed (a new addition just for me) and fell into a very deep sleep.

In what seemed like less than a minute, I awoke to the strains of Frankie Laine softly singing "Rose of Malaya," and the record was stuck. I could also hear water running somewhere!

"All my life I shall remem click, click, click…

All my life I shall remem click, click, click...
All my life I shall remem click, click, click... "
Sitting up and squinting, I attempted to get my eyes focused through the darkness: There stood Eddie, butt naked, holding his dick and spraying piss on the record player as Frankie Laine crooned.

Turning over I went back to sleep.

We always started back to school in North Little Rock on the first Monday after Labor Day. But this year, we were going to High School. Lots of things were different in tenth grade. To begin with, you got to pick what classes you wanted to take, you had to buy books, and everybody looked and acted real grown up, especially Eddie and Me.

Boys wore blue jeans, starched short sleeve shirts, white socks and penny loafers. At least the real boys. Sissies wore saddle oxfords.

Trashy girls wore tight skirts with a back-pleat at the knee, and tight sweaters with nylon scarves tied at the neck, Poodle cuts, and bustle backs, but never pony tails. Sometimes, they even wore high heels.

Nice girls usually wore full skirts over starched horsehair crinolines, sweaters dyed to match, ballerina flats or saddle oxfords. Charm bracelets, and pony-tails! Of course!

All the girls clutched their books to their chest with one hand. Most of the boys held their books in one hand, hanging them casually (and coolly) alongside their hip.

Now sometimes the boys who wore saddle oxfords held their books clutched to their chests, just like the girls. We sure had our opinions about them.

Lunch in the cafeteria was a quarter, but for the same price you could get a burger and a coke at the "Dog House." Located on the corner just across the street from the High school, the small cafe was a place where, we could listen to the juke box, smoke a cigarette, or demonstrate our maturity by sticking up our noses at the kids who ate in the cafeteria.

I knew his name was James Knowland. This was also his first year in High school, but it was his first year in Arkansas, too. His step-daddy was stationed at the new Air Force base in Jacksonville and they'd just been transferred in.

James was hard to miss because of the size of his nose. He looked as if his entire body had been sucked into a vacuum and only his nose had saved him. Sort of a teachers' pet, James was always raising his hand, doing homework, and making good grades.

Despite all that, James still seemed kinda like a regular guy. He always spoke to everyone, even asking about their folks, or how a particular class was going. He could even remember Janice's name. Sometimes, he'd even buy a guy a coke or something. One time, he mentioned something about getting a military pension or something from his dead daddy. Eddie and I had been hanging out with him for the last few weeks, at least at school.

He and Eddie were already eating when I got to the Dog House, so I went to the counter and got a bag of peanuts and an RC. As I sat down emptying the bag of Planters into my RC, Eddie said "James has his step-daddy's car tonight. Wanna go to the Skyline?"

"I ain't got no money."

"Shit, I ain't either, but we can sneak in."

Dodging clotheslines we crossed the backyards at Silver City Court, and headed towards the Pike where we were gonna hitch a ride out to Knowland's.

"Hey Wilson, where y'all headed?"

It was Tommy from my Latin class. Tall and athletic, Tommy had very curly blonde hair, and all the girls thought he was cute. He sat right across from me, and whenever we broke into groups or there was any sort of exercise he always ended up in my group. Tommy seemed to understand all that Latin crap and would let me copy his homework. I kinda liked him.

Tommy and his folks lived in the Courts too, just like Eddie and them.

"We're goin over to James Knowland's and then sneakin' inta the Skyline."

Y'all think it'd be OK if I went?"

"Sure," said Eddie. What the hell did he care? It wasn't his car.

"Let me tell my Momma, and then we can go."

Eddie and I walked ahead slowly, waiting for Tommy to catch up to us. We could tell by the slamming of a screen door that he wasn't far behind.

"Y'all sure it's OK?"

"Ol Knowland won't mind. He's all right."

Tommy got us a ride the first time he stuck out his thumb. He and I were left to ride in the back of the truck of course. Eddie as usual leaped into the front seat beside the driver. He always got the front seat.

I could see him through the little window, smoking, talking to the driver and acting like a big shit. When the driver slowed at 47th. Street we hopped out of the back of the truck, and after saying thanks began the long steep climb up the hill to Knowland's house.

"You still dating Carolee?" Tommy asked Eddie.

"Huh!" I snuffed. "He ain't gonna quit her until he gits some of that fat pussy."

"Wilson, you are a real asshole." Eddie said as we walked up to Knowland's front porch.

"Hi Miz Corkran, this here's Tommy."

"Hello Tommy. Are you in the same grade as James?"

"Yes, ma'am" I answered. "He's in our Latin class."

"Thank you, George."

Pulling off the road in Levy Knowland opened the trunk of Volta's car for us to get into. Eddie waited until Tommy and I crawled in first, then he crawled in on top of us. After slamming the lid, James drove alone the last block up to the Drive In. We were jammed tight against each other, and It was hotter'n shit in the trunk.

Plus, that fucking Eddie seemed to be getting heavier by the minute. I attempted several times to push him off, but each new attempt brought either a "Goddammit" or a threat of a fart. It seemed like it took forever until we heard the girl at the booth take Knowland's quarter and felt the car begin its climb up to the balconies.

"What the fuck took so long? I thought I wuz gonna pass clean out." Eddie complained as the trunk lid finally opened and the cool air rushed in.

"There was a long line, and they looked at me funny, I think they might still be watching."

Knowland was such a chicken shit !

And, wouldn't you know it? Eddie flounced right to the front seat again so Tommy and I spent the first few minutes of the show trying to see the screen around his big head. Finally in desperation we moved down to the theater seats at the concession stand. The feature that night was "Unchained Melody." It was about a football player who did something wrong, then got thrown into prison. It was kinda mushy but had a real good song.

"Time goes by so slowly,
and time can mean so much.
I need your love, I need your love,
Go-odd speed your love to me"

The sticky cold juice of the watermelon was running down all our faces, but it was so sweet and refreshing that no one seemed to mind. We had deserted the indoor summer heat for whatever small relief we were able to find on the front porch. Momma, Neecy and Betty sat swinging back and forth in the swing. J.W. had brought a chair from the kitchen and was leaning on its back legs against the wall. Sitting alone on the edge of the porch, I let my legs dangle into the darkness. As we ate the melon, we talked quietly, watching the cars as they turned off Pike Avenue and headed down Fiftieth Street.

There were no street lights this far out of town, so whenever a car turned onto the street its headlights would suddenly illuminate the entire summer road and sometimes creatures caught midstream in their attempt to cross the blacktop unnoticed. A possum, Raccoons, snakes, and occasionally some very large tarantulas could be seen glowing in the dazzling light. The snakes and tarantulas would always stir some "Oh Lordees" or "ooo-wee's" from Momma and the girls.

J.W. and I, of course, were made of much rougher stuff. It really was a little bit creepy though. I'd sure as shit hate for any of those things to get on me.

Ever since Betty's divorce from Carl she and the babies had been living with us on Fiftieth. It had been several months, before she had finally been able to get a regular job working at Huggin's Drug Store down in Levy. The house on Fiftieth was a little crowded but none of us seemed to mind. We were all secretly relieved that we would never have to lay eyes on Carl's sorry ass again. None of us ever mentioned him, and, except for the babies there was no evidence that he had ever even existed. There sure wasn't any child support.

Betty had been dating Adam for the last two weeks. He was on leave from the Marines in California, and he and Betty had run into each other at the drugstore. They had been in grade school and then junior high together, so Adam didn't seem strange to us, but more like an old friend. Adam's pale skin was tanned from the California sun, and his short cropped red hair glowed like flame.

Each time you met Adam his mischievous blue eyes seemed as though he had just been caught in mid-prank. The babies liked Adam a lot, and so did we. Adam was driving his Daddy's Bel-Air while he was on leave. He and Betty had even taken me and Neecy to the show with them once.

"Adam asked me to come to California with him." Betty said.

"I can't take care of them babies." Momma replied.

"I know that Momma, but he asked me to get married."

The dark silence was suddenly interrupted by headlights. Kind of whopper-jawed, the lights illuminated just the right side of the road and the lower limbs of the overhanging trees.

"Don't be silly, sister. You just got yourself a good steady job." This from the usually silent J.W.

"Y'all don't understand. I just feel like I need to get out of Arkansas. There's no way to for me to get ahead here, and I'm afraid Carl will come back!"

"How long would you be staying?"

"I don't know, Momma. it would depend on Adam and what happens with the Marines. He has two more years to go on his enlistment."

"Where would y'all be at?"

"He's at Camp Pendleton now, somewhere south of Los Angeles at a town called Oceanside. I guess we would be near there."

"How you planning on getting' there?"

"I heard they pay you to drive cars out there so they can sell them for more money, and I figured I'd do that."

"I never heard of that." said J.W.

"Well, I already looked into it. They pay for the gas and give you $20 a day, but it's only for one way."

"Are you sure it's okay?"

"It was in the Arkansas *Democrat*. They allow you five days to get there, but I figure if I drive straight through I can be there in about two or three days."

"Why Lordee, Sister, you can't stay up for two days and nights without a wink of sleep. You might doze off and have a wreck."

"I think it'd be all right, Momma. That way I'd be there quick and have some extra money to rent a place, and I'll drink plenty of coffee and take me some No-Doz."

"What about the babies Hon?" Momma asked.

"I don't know, but I figger I'll have to leave em here for a while"

"Sister, we don't have no money or no way to take care of little ones."

"Well, I guess I'll just have to board them at the orphanage then!"

"Oh no!" Neecy squawled, "They eat babies out there!"

"Oh, they don't neither. Where do y'all hear all that stuff?"

"Everybody knows it." I said.

"Sister, if you don't pay they'll give your babies away!"

"Well, I'm going, that's all there is to it, and I guess I'll just have to get the money somehow."

"Just don't come lookin' to us when you can't pay."

"Now y'all don't fuss." J.W. said. "We'll figure something out."

That's what he always said, and he always was able to figure something out!

J.W. was definitely not a hollerer. Quietly and calmly ask

questions getting the details, think them over, and then reach a decision no matter what the problem. Usually he was right of course, and when he wasn't he'd just admit it and figure out a new solution. The girls called him Daddy and had learned to love him deeply. I didn't call him Daddy, but whenever I needed something or there was a problem I'd always go to him first. He was more logical than Momma.

"When you plannin' on leavin'?" asked J.W.

"The first week of June. They'd be able to hire kids at the drugstore then and I'd most likely lose my job anyways."

I loved biscuits and gravy, but the first Monday morning in May, I could hardly taste them. J.W. had driven Betty to work at the drug store earlier, and it was just him, Momma, Neecy and me.

"If Sister Jo says it's OK, can I go to California with her?"

"Son, eat your breakfast and don't be crazy."

"Naw Momma, really. Can I go? I'll help her stay awake, or I can drive a little."

"We'll talk about it later."

"Aw Momma, please! I don't never get to go nowhere."

"Oh all right, but just hush up and eat."

I had run almost the whole way to the drugstore to persuade Betty. I knew that if Momma talked to her before I did, then there wasn't a chance in hell for me to be California bound this year.

"And Sister Jo, I can help you stay awake, and I won't eat a thing, and I can even drive so's you can rest."

"An I can help drive, an I'll talk so you don't go to sleep, an help you clean when y'all rent a place, and watch the babies when they come out, and I promise not to be no trouble."

"Did Momma really say you could go?"

"Cross my heart."

"Well, we'll see."

"Naw, promise…Pleaseeeeeeeee, oh pretty please!"

"Well, how'd you get back here in time for school?"

"The Trailways is only $18 dollars, I already called."

"Oh well, I guess it'd be all right if Momma says so."

The student council was having a sock hop at the Boy's club the Saturday night before Mothers day, and Eddie and I had gone late to avoid paying. They charged a quarter, but usually a few minutes after the dance started the student council members would drift on into the party leaving the door unattended.

I danced the first couple of times with Jewel, and after that several other girls started asking me to dance. Eddie on the other hand stood in the corner with some other guys cussing and making fun of the dancers. After an hour or so he came over and asked:

"You ready to go?"

"Naw, why you wanta leave so early?'

"I'm tired of this shit, and I'm hungry!"

"What you givin your Momma for Mothers Day?" Eddie asked.

"Probly nothin', I ain't got no money"

We were passing Owens's funeral home where they had put out huge pots of caladiums, lining the sidewalk in front of the building. They had even thoughtfully wrapped each pot in gold foil and tied it with a big red bow.

It was almost midnight, and after we had liberated the best of the undertaker's caladiums, we decided it would be prudent to choose a new route home. Walking through Niggertown we were able to avoid street lights and the law.

"Why you don't ask Betty if I can go with y'all to California?"

"Aw, man, I don't know. She's liable to change her mind if I show out."

We changed arms with the pots. The caladiums were getting heavy.

"Come on...There'd be plenty of room, and I'll pay my own way!"

"Huh! Where'd you get any money?"

"Momma said she'd give me forty dollars, and after we get there I could go stay with my Momma's aunt in Compton."

"Where's that?"

"I don't know, but she said it'd be okay for the summer."

We changed arms once again. Those damn caladiums really were heavy.

"Aw Sister Jo, come on. He won't be no trouble."

"Well, I guess I can call his Momma and see what she says."

We were eating Mother's Day dinner. Betty had cooked and it was pretty good. At least it wasn't Momma's cookin'. Momma did lots of things good, but nobody ever said she was any kind of cook. She thought that if it was hot and tender and had lots of salt it was "good and good for you."

When food left Momma's stove it had been boiled or fried until it was either grey-green or black, leaving little clue as to what it had once been. She kept an old can on the stove for bacon drippings and the residue from anything she fried was added to the can after each meal.

Somehow that can never seemed to get full.

A big dollop of the drippings always preceded anything into her frying pan, and occasionally whatever pan was going into the oven.

The caladium had been a suspicious success. Momma thanked me with a raised eyebrow and a very doubtful expression.

Betty had been assigned a 53 Pontiac coupe for the trip to California. Painted sea foam green, anything on the car that could be chrome plated was. It was difficult to tell if it was a green car with chrome trim, or a chrome car with green trim. I had never seen a more beautiful automobile.

Betty said we were leaving at dawn, so after a hasty good-bye to Nellie and the boys, Eddie, his one small suitcase and I hitchhiked to Levy where we were spending the night. Neither one of us had slept very much. Eddie had never been out of Arkansas, and I had only been as far as Memphis.

When Betty called, "Wake up boys, its time." we were already up and half dressed.

For several hours, almost the only sound had been the wind over the Pontiac. The excitement, added to the apprehension of what we'd find out West, had given me a clammy sweat. The sweat along with the silence had lasted almost all the way to Fort Smith. It was there that we would cross over into Oklahoma.

When we left the house Eddie hadn't said a word as I grabbed the front seat and pulled it forward to let him in the back seat, but the "eat shit" look he gave me almost had a smell.

"Y'all want to stop and pee and git a cold drink, before we cross over?" Sister Jo asked.

"Naw," we agreed "Let's go on."

"Welcome to Oklahoma" said the sign..."I'm hungry." said Eddie.

There were no golden arches in those days, so we stopped at a filling station, bought gas and RC's then we unfolded the waxed paper, and gobbled down the pressed ham and Miracle Whip sandwiches Betty had made the night before.

"How far is it now? " Eddie asked.

"It's just as far as it is." was the only answer Betty was prepared to give. I said. "We still got all of Oklahoma, Texas, New Mexico, Arizona and then all of California to cross."

"How do you know, Mr. Smartass."

"Cause I studied fore we left, butthead."

"Now Sonny, stop your cussin."

"Yeah Sonny, stop your cussin." he punched my shoulder.

"Cuss this" I said raising one cheek and giving them both a huge pressed ham fart.

"Aw shit" moaned Eddie.

"Y'all better stop it right now, you hear, or I'll drop y'all at the Trailways."

That silenced us both almost as far as Tulsa.

Swinging onto the toll road in Tulsa, we could see the lights of Oklahoma City off in the distance. There stood the tallest building Eddie and I had ever seen, and it was lit at the top. The lights changed colors! Blue, then red, then green. Exceptional!

At Oklahoma City we caught Route 66 which would take us all the way to California. By now we were getting tired and a little cranky, and the pressed ham sandwiches were beginning to get a little old.

We had eaten them again at suppertime. By then the ham had gone a little slick, and the bread was kinda wet and mushy.

"Lordee this is flat land," Betty said as we entered the Texas panhandle.

It was getting close to midnight, and the two stops for coffee had not kept either Eddie or me awake and alert for very long. We had both been dozing fitfully when she spoke:

"Hon, let's talk a little, I'm getting drowsy."

"Okay."

"I sure hope them kids are all right at the orphanage. I paid the first month already, and Adam said he'd give me the money for next month when we get to Oceanside."

"Why'nt you bring them?"

"Lord honey, you don't know what's gonna happen. I may not get work, or Adam could get shipped out."

"But you and me coulda took care of em."

"Sonny, it's better this way."

"I don't see why Momma and them couldn'ta kept em."

The silence was interrupted only by Eddies snoring, and the sound of the cool night wind whistling over the sleek chrome Pontiac.

"Look way up yonder, do you think that's a city?"

"I don't know, but it sure is something ain't it."

"Huh...what...where're...we at?"

"Well, look who's up."

"We just crossed over into Texas."

"When we gonna eat? I'm hungry."

"They's more pressed ham."

"Naw, I'm tired of that crap, let's get a hamburger or somethin'."

"Yeah, sister me too!"

"Y'all know we ain't got no money to waste."

"Shit, I'll pay." said Eddie.

We inhaled the greasy burgers and fries, and in an exhausted stupor fell back into the Pontiac. It seemed like it took forever to get across Texas. I woke up first, and looking over I caught Betty's eye, smiling she reached across and patted me on the shoulder.

"Oh, my mouth feels like the russian army took a shit in it!"

"Good morning eddie." said Betty.

"When we stopping? I got to pee, and I'm hungry."

"We aren't far from New Mexico, you reckon you can wait till then?"

"For eating yeah, but I gotta pee right now."

Unnoticed in the darkness the terrain had gone from flat prairie to draws and mesas. There were very few trees visible, and the ground was now covered in tumbleweed and some sort of low cactus. Betty pulled to the Pontiac over and Eddie and I wandered over to a small mesquite bush and stepping behind it took a pee.

"How far you think it is?" he asked.

"I figure we're about halfway there now. Why?"

"Oh no reason asshole, I just thought I'd ask for something to do."

"I hope Betty will stop for breakfast soon, I'm getting a little hungry myself."

"Y'all come on now, we got to get going." Betty yelled from the car.

If Texas was flat, New Mexico was anything but. The land went from scrub to red clay, until even the rocks and hills seemed to be the same. In just a few miles we had gone from shallow draws to deep Canyons and from mesas to towering Buttes. Even the occasional cactus, seemed like a visitor to this barren land, which looked unable to sustain any but the most meager plants and the hardiest of animals.

By the time we got to Gallup I had decided that everything in this state, including the people, was made of exactly the same ingredient. Red dust. A couple of times off in the distance we could see Pueblos built into the sides of some of the taller cliffs. There were even places where Tee Pees sat beside the road, and from which, what appeared to be real Indians were selling souvenirs.

After a breakfast of pancakes and sausage, we were fortified for the day, and headed on towards Arizona.

"You wanta drive for a little while Sonny?"

"Yeah, that'd be great Sis."

"Why'nt you let me drive Betty?"

"No Eddie, I think it'll be better if Sonny drives. But, I'm gonna sleep for a while, so you can ride up in front."

"Wake up Sis." I said as the sign welcoming us to Arizona appeared beside the road.

"What's wrong? Is there some sort of a problem?"

"Naw, were coming up on Arizona and I wanted to know what to do."

"Well, you better pull over and let me drive, in case they stop us."

"Yeah, they might put your ass in jail." said Eddie.

"Shut up jerk."

"Y'all hush, go ahead and pull on over now Sonny."

I got out and let Betty in on the drivers' side, but when I went around Eddie refused to get out of the front seat.

"You got to set up her most of the way, so it's my turn now."

"Get your but in the back seat Eddie."

"I ain't gonna do it."

"Y'all don't fight. Sonny, just get in the back for a little while. We'll be stopping soon anyway."

"Alright, but just till the next stop." I said glaring at Eddie and mouthing *asshole* as I slid into the back seat.

From the border it seemed not to take too long before we were almost through Arizona. Eddie had actually opened the door and gotten into the back after we stopped for lunch in Flagstaff.

"Arizona don't favor shit," Eddie stated sort of matter of factly, and I had to agree. Lacking the color of New Mexico or Texas, what mountains it had were rocky and grey.

"I'm gonna go pee and get another drank of water. Wanna go?" I said as I rose up to my knees and squinted from the glare of the sun on the waves rolling ashore.

Eddie rolled over onto his back in the sand, without answering. We entered California with the sunrise at our backs. To me, the whole state seemed to be shrouded in a golden mist that touched everything, including the people.

In what seemed like a very short time after leaving the Welcome to California sign in the rear view mirror, and the check for fruits and vegetables at the border, the Golden State had been transformed. At first a dusty gray and tan desert, giving way to low lying golden hills,

California soon became small pale green mountains topped by neat stucco homes with clay roofs.

"Y'all stay here, and I'll be back later." Betty said as she let us out near the pier on the beach at Oceanside. Camp Pendleton was just a few miles east of the ocean, and Betty had gone off to find Adam.

Changing into our swim trunks in the dank smelly men's room, we stepped gingerly over the puddles on the floor as we walked into the intense glow of the brilliant southern California sun.

The addictive smell of salt and suntan lotion, fanned by the Pacific breeze and the sounds of the ocean, almost made us forget our pasty grub color and our shapeless bodies.

Everywhere you looked there were golden people. Their hair, their skin, and sometimes, it seemed as if even their eyes were flecked with particles of sunlight. I had never seen anything so foreign, or as lovely.

It was midmorning, and the relentless sun was beginning to bear down on our delicate, winter white, hillbilly skins.

This was the third or fourth time I had been to pee. I don't know if I really had to go, or if the cool shade in the bathroom and the water cooler just outside its door kept beckoning me back.

Returning to a large indentation in the sand where Eddie had been, I discovered there was no one there. I looked every which way, but there was no sign of him anywhere. Afraid to leave to search for him and getting us both lost, I plopped angrily down onto the steaming sand.

"Goddammit, we're supposed to stay together and not run off from each other." I said when he finally reappeared.

I think I was madder about his leaving me alone than I was about him eating without me. He said he had just taken a walk, but the mustard on his chin made me a little suspicious.

Our skin had slowly changed from white to pink, then rapidly turned to an angry red and was now beginning to tighten as sundown approached and Betty finally returned.

"We're stayin' in a motel tonight, and then tomorrow Sonny, we'll have to find a place. And Eddie, you have to call your aunt and find out what bus you need to catch to get to her house."

"Aw shoot, Sis, why can't he stay with us?"

"Now, George, you know he can't. We've already made plans."

By the time Eddie boarded the Trailways bus to Compton I had begun to itch and burn. By the time we drove to the small apartment Betty and Adam had rented that afternoon, the pain from the sunburn had become s almost unbearable. The apartment had a combination living room and kitchen, and a bedroom with a bath.

It appeared that at one time it had been a motel, but they had converted one of the bathrooms to a Pullman kitchen and opened a door between the rooms.

I barely remember us meeting Adam, because I was in such a daze from the sunburns pain. Betty spent most of the afternoon right on until evening smoothing condensed milk over my sunburned skin until I fell thankfully into an exhausted sleep.

The next few days were a blur, except for Adams getting up each morning at 4:30, making coffee on the stove at the end of my bed, and leaving for the base.

When the pain of the sunburn finally began to subside I was able to begin my exploration of Fallbrook.

The small farming town was nestled in a picture perfect valley between hills striped with groves, and trees dotted with avocados or lemons. The main road left Camp Pendleton doglegging right in the middle of Fallbrook where a small motel, a neighborhood grocery, and a picture show were the entire downtown business district. Showing Spanish language films on Thursday and Friday nights, the action was terrific, but the dialogue was totally lost to me.

Hiding from the road, concealed behind the motel and the playground, there was a very small, very scruffy, half empty trailer park.

There was no pool at the motel, and the small playground was shrouded by a grove of huge eucalyptus trees, which like me also seemed to be peeling their sunburns. In the center of the playground, overlooking the road, there sat an ancient glider whose oilcloth canopy and floral upholstery had long since faded to gray green. I spent most of my first evenings in Fallbrook sitting on the glider, waiting for exhaustion and loneliness to force me inside to sleep.

Betty and Adam's marriage ceremony (I hesitate to call it a wedding) was a very simple one. Several marines and a few of their wives made up the wedding party. The dress was sort of "catch as catch can," except for the marines. The enlisted men and the Officers all looked splendid in their dress uniforms.

The only officer in attendance, besides the chaplain, was Adam's company commander.

The Commander, a very stern looking man with exceptionally white teeth, appeared to be looking down on the entire proceedings, ready to discipline any breach of etiquette.

Adam in his dress blues looked like a recruiting ad, and Betty fairly sparkled. In the few days we had been in California a sunny glow had found its way onto her cheeks, and a certain lightness that hadn't been there since she had married Carl, now re-illuminated her spirit

"Hi, I'm Rex. I'll bet you're Adam's new brother in law Sonny."

"Yeah." I mumbled, as I shyly faced the floor.

"He's been talkin' a lot about y'all, and how excited he is that you'll be stayin' for the summer."

"Yeah, I gotta go back for school."

"Well it's a long time to Labor Day Sonny. Maybe we can do somethin' fun together. What do you wanna do while you're out here?"

"I told everyone that I wuz gonna go to Hollywood.'"

"Well, then you are!"

Rex looked just like Tab Hunter to me. Tall and blonde with blue eyes, he and his older brother Kenneth had joined the marines two years earlier when Rex was just 16. Back in Corsicana, Texas on boot leave Kenneth married his high school sweetheart Carol who had returned to California with them when their leave was up. Their brand new baby boy was the only person at the wedding younger than me.

"Now Rex, don't you be teaching this young boy no bad stuff. Hi,

I'm Carol, Rex's sister in law, and I'll just bet you're Sonny."

"My real names George, but they all call me Sonny."

"Well then, we're gonna call you Sonny too!"

"Here Hon, will you hold the baby while I go pee?" Carol said shoving the blonde haired infant into my arms.

Rex sat by me through the entire ceremony and was treating me as if I was as grown up as him. He asked me questions about Arkansas, Betty and our family. He told me about life in Texas, riding horses, hunting wild hogs, and about being in the Marines.

By the time Carol got back from peeing, Rex and I had already begun a friendship, and together we were planning our trip to Hollywood that coming Saturday.

While seeing Hollywood was one of my dreams come true, I was even more thrilled to find out that Rex, along with Kenneth and Carol were living in the same motel that we were in.

As the wedding party was winding down, the chaplain, who had been very friendly, asked me if I wanted to go spend the night at his Beach house. He said that Betty and Adam would probably appreciate some time alone. I eagerly accepted, said bye to Betty, Adam and Rex, and we were off to the Beach.

I had never known anyone who lived in as nice a house, or who lived as well as the Father. His apartment was on the second floor of a building in Oceanside, and was right on the beach. Each room had a view of the Pacific, and while I couldn't see it in the dark, I could hear it. Sometimes sound is much more provocative than sight.

"This is your room." he said and pulled the door closed, leaving me alone.

Carefully lying across the bed I enjoyed the sensation of being lulled into sleep by the sound of the waves hitting the beach and the softness of the sheets. In what seemed like just a few minutes there was a knock at the door telling me that breakfast was ready. Suddenly very hungry, I sat up to find that a robe had been laid across the foot of the bed, and slippers on the floor.

After a meal of ham and eggs and strawberries in cream, I followed him into the surf where we let the waves continue to awaken us.

The mist was thick and damp without a trace of the heat that Eddie and I had experienced just two days earlier. I felt as if I had been transported into a new and somehow far better place.

Rex was as good as his word. He knocked on our door first thing on Saturday and we were off to Hollywood. The trip was in many ways the most exotic, and yet somehow one of the most natural things I had ever done. More than a city, Hollywood was an attitude. The most exciting place I had ever imagined, it lived up to its promise.

That day, I saw people and things, that would bring me back to Hollywood boulevard many times, years later when I was in the Navy and stationed in San Diego. First, Rex took me to Griffith Park, and the planetarium which I would later recognize in the movie "A Rebel Without a Cause." Then, we spent an hour at Pershing Square.

We walked around the square, from one soapbox or park bench to another, listening to the outrageous excesses of one radical after another, each one giving you their opinion on everything from Communism to Flying saucers.

We examined the flora and fauna of Hollywood boulevard, waiting to be discovered at Hollywood and Vine. Viewing each passing luxury car with raised eyebrows, we wondered what famous person might be riding in the back seat, or what important meeting they might be on their way to.

If the days in Fallbrook became a little tedious I do not remember, for my mind has added a golden haze to the perfectly shaped and aligned hills, to the solitary walks at dusk down narrow dirt roads linking the tile roofed and azalea trimmed houses, each perched on it's own hilltop.

This glow has extended itself to cover attending Spanish language movies at the little theater, and the deep affection I felt for this little town, and especially those kind strangers.

Unlike the days, the nights in Fallbrook seemed ablaze with excitement. Most of the time Adam would have some buddies over who told us exciting stories of combat and life in the Corps. Rex or the chaplain would often have chosen some terrific destination, or planned some sort of event for me.

We went to the beach at Malibu, or drove into the mountains above Hollywood and Los Angeles. Once with the chaplain, I even went to Venice and saw the California that easterners only imagine.

And frequently, there were trips to the local bar with Rex, where I was allowed to sip beer from his glass, and he'd give me money for the jukebox or to play shuffleboard.

"There's a yellow rose in Texas that I am goin to see,
No body else could miss her, not half as much as me."
She cried so when I left her, it liked to broke my heart
Before I knew it the summer was over.

I could hardly bear to say goodbye to Rex and the chaplain, but even more difficult was leaving my Sister who up until now had not been my friend, only my sister. I spent that last Friday night at the chaplain's house, well really at the beach by his house. Eating sandwiches we watched the sunset into the Pacific.

We talked a lot about keeping in touch, and my returning the next summer. It seemed like it might really happen. On Saturday morning, I was barely able to hold back the tears until I was in the trailer.

I didn't know how to say goodbye to Rex. It was different with him, he was my age (well almost), and he liked all the same things I did. He also understood the difficulty. He put out his hand and took mine, then holding it in his he put his other arm around my shoulder and drew me to him for a long hug. Releasing me he stood back and looked into my eyes.

"Sonny, I'm goin' to remember you forever! I know we probably ain't ever goin to see each other again, so let's not make no promises we can't keep. But I do swear that I'll always remember you and think of you everyday. Will you think of me?"

The Greyhound arrived in Little Rock on Wednesday before Labor Day, and school started the very next Tuesday.

The California summer had tanned my skin, gotten rid of some unwelcome baby fat, and opened my eyes.

I was a much different boy than when I left North Little Rock.

Taller, skinnier, and at least in my mind, a great deal more mature than I had been before.

A summer away from Momma and a summer spent being treated as an adult had given me a certain degree of coolness, and new confidence.

I had learned that I was not inferior, I was no longer shy, and for the first time in my life I felt as if I really might have a chance.

I also had come to realize that just as soon as I could, somehow I would leave Arkansas and my life there for whatever I was able to find, somewhere, anywhere else.

J.W. offered to drive me and Neecy to school so we could be early on the first day. She was able to walk the two blocks from high school to Jefferson Davis Junior High, so he didn't have to make but one stop.

Perhaps something had been going around that summer. Because, while I had been in California growing up, Janice (no longer Neecy) had also done a little growing on her own.

She had lost some of her own baby fat, got the beginning of a figure, and was developing her own style. She was rapidly turning into a very good looking teenager. She had also found a whole new group of girlfriends who weren't too bad looking either.

"Hey Wilson, wait up" Eddie hollered as I reached for the door to the music building. We hadn't seen each other since we returned from California.

"You takin' choir too?" he asked.

"Yeah, I heard it ain't got no homework."

"When'd you get back?"

"The other day'"

"You git any California pussy?" he laughed loudly.

"Fuck you."

"I got some regular." he lied.

The bedraggled football jacket was now so small that it barely covered his sides, and there was no way in hell it could ever have been buttoned. Eddie had obviously gained a lot of weight over the summer. All of his clothes, and even his skin seemed too tight.

Compared to him, I thought I looked real good. I was wearing a new plaid shirt-Jac Rex had given me as I had boarded the Greyhound in Fallbrook, and Momma had bought me a new pair of jeans that were almost too tight. The shirt-Jac fit snug at the waist, had short sleeves and a turned up collar, and it really seemed to set me off.

I not only felt different from when I had left Arkansas. I looked different.

"Y'all settle down now, class." Ms. Birdsong said as we entered the already full choir room. The desks were set onto three tiers so she was able to see each face, and hear each voice clearly from her position at the piano.

The music building was new, so it still had a nice smell of wood and wax. The choir and the band shared the building, each with its own large practice room with walls of windows on two sides.

The new building sat on a little knoll to the west of the main school building, and when you were there you felt removed, like you were somewhere else.

As I slid in beside Eddie, he lifted up one side of his butt and gave us a huge fart.

Pandemonium followed.

As the laughter stopped Ms. Birdsong began: "I cannot imagine what sort of upbringing a person has had that would do this sort of thing. I require that you all act like ladies and gentlemen, and I will not tolerate any other sort of indecent behavior from anyone. Should you feel that you are unable to act accordingly, it would be best that you tell me now, so we can terminate your participation in choir prior to my terminating it for you. Mr. Wilson, please see me in my office after practice. If there are no further questions, we will begin:

Please give me an "A."

Because my face was the reddest, she assumed it had been me. I tried to blame Eddie, but nevertheless I was the one who was told to report for 30 minutes detention when school let out.

Leaving Miss Birdsongs office I noticed Eddie standing in the pit smoking. A stand of bushes to the rear end of the Music building, the pit was where boys were allowed to smoke. Ignoring his wave I walked on to my next class.

For the rest of the day, when I saw Eddie I didn't speak, and at lunch I refused to sit with him at the Dog House, choosing instead to sit with Hal and Celinda.

"Hey Wilson, want a ride?" It was James.

"Yeah thanks, how come you're here so late?" I asked as I slid into the shotgun seat of the cigar shaped' 49 Ford.

"I was at a student body meeting."

"Ass kisser."

"Fuck you. How come you're still here?" He asked.

"Eddie caused me to get detention"

Turning right onto Railroad Avenue, he said. "I'm running for vice president this year. You want to help me?"

The school elections were in the spring.

"Sure." I said. Spring was a long way off.

As James turned left onto Fiftieth, he said "You wanta come over and eat supper at my house? Then we can go over to Little Rock and cruise Snappy's."

"Sure."

"Do you hafta tell your parents?"

"Naw, they ain't home."

The food was really good, and they always treated me real nice. There was lots of laughing and telling of stories about Cissy's childhood and growing up in Louisiana.

We heard about "Shivaree's, fais do do's, eating crawfish in Breaux Bridge, and they even claimed that Longfellow's "Evangeline" was buried somewhere down there.

James's Daddy was dead just like mine. He had been killed in Korea when James was just a kid. Apparently "Volta D" had been stationed with James's daddy so it just seemed natural for him to replace him.

We had taken to calling James's Momma "Cissy" and his step daddy "Volta D." Cissy's Momma had the same funny accent as her daughter and recently had come up from Louisiana for an extended visit.

Cissy had made beef cubes in gravy, served over rice. We only ate rice for breakfast at home, but it was still real good, and I ate a whole lot. Soon as we finished "Cissys" fabulous lemon meringue pie we were off to Snappy's.

Snappy Service was a drive-in across the river in Little Rock where you placed your order through a speaker, then girls on roller-skates delivered it to your car. Most of the time the kids didn't have any money to eat, so they'd just cruise round and round with their radios blaring, seeing who else was cruising.

"Hey dipshit," Eddie hollered as we passed. He was with Robby Turner. I shot him a finger as James and I made the turn.

That Saturday we were going to get together and plan James's campaign. Eddie and Tommy had also been drafted into helping. Cissy said she would cook supper, and make us a blackberry cobbler, but first, we'd have to go out to Camp Robinson and pick her some blackberries. Cissy and Volta drove us out to the camp, but James's Granny said she was feeling a little poorly so she stayed home.

Three or four hours later when we returned home with our pails of blackberries it was very obvious that something was bad wrong with James's Granny. Granny was sort of slung back across the couch and there was a hollow glassy look in her eyes. On the floor at the end of the sofa were the remains of a 12 pack of Dr. Tichenor's Antiseptic.

A vile smelling concoction of 17% alcohol and some other things that, at least according to the good Doctor, promised fresh breath, long life, and some other bullshit.

As it turned out, Granny was addicted to Dr. Tichenor's, and the reason they lived in that small town in Louisiana was that there wasn't anyplace there that sold the product. While we'd been out picking berries Granny had ordered up a case of the Magic elixir from Huggin's drug store, and was now pie-eyed, knee-walking, ass-wallering drunk.

Cissy went to squawling and whining, "Now Momma, you know that stuff ain't no good for you."

"I don't know what you mean Cissy. I ain't done nothing, cept take a little bit of tonic for my condition. Y'all boys find any berries?"

"Momma, you ought to go on to bed now."

"I ain't sleepy, Cissy. Y'all was gone a long time boys. I bet y'all have to pee real bad."

"Now Momma, you leave them boys alone."

"Back when I'uz a girl we'd take us a coke bottle to pee in."

Eddie, Tommy and me started giggling, but James and his Momma weren't very amused.

"I bet I can still pee in a bottle if I want to. Y'all wanna bet."

"Aw Momma, please go on to bed."

Before any one could say anything or make an attempt to stop her, she'd grabbed up one of the Dr. Tichenor's bottles, extended her right arm as far out and down as she could, hiked up her skirt and proceeded to shoot a stream of pee all over the corner of the sofa, onto the carpet, and on Cissy's and James's legs as they tried to wrestle the bottle away from her and get her skirt down. After all was said and done, I believe a few drops actually did end up in the Dr. Tichenor's bottle.

The three of us were collapsed with laughter, falling all over the porch as Cissy was finally able to get her protesting Mother to bed.

"Y'all shut-up laughing goddammit, she didn't mean nothin." James said.

After order was restored, and supper served, we finally got back to campaign business and stopped any further discussion of Granny's unusual talent. By the way, the cobbler was excellent!

The Boys Club at 13th and Main Street had a dance every Friday night open only to the kids in High School. Since it was free we always went. It was never dates; we just went as a group. Jewel and I usually danced together, so we had begun to develop a little bit of style.

We were even planning on getting onto the 5 P.M. Dance Show in Little Rock. Eddie just danced with whoever he could find.

One winter night James, Eddie, and I were planning on going to the Boys Club for the dance. Eddie was spending the night at my house, and James was supposed to come over and pick us up in his car after supper. It hadn't looked like snow when school let out, but before we got home to 50th.it had begun to fall with a vengeance. I was in my heavy old green car coat and as usual Eddie was wearing his by now, way too small, 4th Street football jacket with the fading letter.

Every step we took it seemed like it was getting colder and we were getting wetter.

By the time we got into the house, the melting snow was beginning to freeze into icy puddles and ice was forming on the tree branches and power lines. We were chilled and damp, but a couple of cans of tamales each and we both had begun to feel a whole lot better. The phone rang, and it was James telling us that Cissy didn't want him driving in this weather, so he was staying home.

As boredom and twilight were setting in we called James back and said we were going to walk over to his house and play cards or some Parcheesi.

The quickest way to James's house from mine was to cut through the woods and then cross over the cemetery. Four blocks down Fiftieth Street to the west the road dead-ended and the woods began. The woods were only about a mile deep, but without any leaves or foliage they seemed very sinister, and in the deepening twilight, they were becoming very dark. Getting closer to the woods I asked Eddie if he thought that maybe we oughta take the much longer (but well lit) route.

"You're scared aintcha?"

"Naw but if we miss the path we could get lost."

"Shit, Wilson, you are a real pussy."

I stepped defiantly into the woods almost at a run, with Eddie following just a few yards behind. The blanket of quiet that accompanies falling snow made the woods more ominous than I had expected. For what seemed an eternity the only sound was the crunching of our high top tennis shoes in the several inches of snow that now covered the frozen ground.

As the weight of the ice increased, the smaller branches of the trees began to droop under the weight, until they would finally snap. Falling to the ground and into the deepening snow with ghostly, almost unearthly thuds, for just a moment the terrifying hush would be broken. All around us it sounded as if some soft-footed giant was running and crashing through the woods.

"Are we goin' the right way?" Eddie asked, as the woods, the cold, and the silence had now begun to take their toll.

"Yeah!" I said, rapidly quickening the pace.

"Fuck Wilson, you're gittin' our asses lost."

"I ain't lost, goddammit. Why don't you lead if you're so fuckin smart?"

Suddenly right before us there was a clearing and we could see through the black skeletons of the trees. There just a few steps away was the cemetery. We had been walking due north through the woods rather than west, and were now at the far back side of the cemetery where the graves were newer and still mounded above the ground. In the deep twilight they looked like rows of bodies that had been covered with white blankets. As we entered the maze of graves, the blowing snow turned to drizzle, and then sleet.

Ice crystals were beginning form on our faces, and our clothes were becoming heavy and sodden. The wind had been steadily increasing since we entered the woods and now its scream was the only sound we were able to hear.

We never discussed exactly why we started running, whether it was to escape the cold and the rain, or something else. But, as if rehearsed, and in perfect unison, we both broke into a full gallop. Quickly we began to cross the cemetery's wet darkness, stumbling and falling across graves, and leaping over tombstones. All the while we were slipping on ice and splashing through the rapidly freezing puddles. And then, finally, sliding down the last icy embankment and leaving the cemetery behind us, we were suddenly returned to the safety of civilization. Street lights now illuminated the last few blocks to James's.

There was still a ways to go however in the freezing sleet and wind. It took constant leaning force to thrust us into the freezing rain and gales seemingly determined to keep us from James's house. The harder we pushed the harder it became, until finally, topping the last rise and turning, we were able to put the wind and the rain to our backs.

Bursting through the door we flew into the welcome warmth of James's house. Without a word Eddie ran past James and Cissy, throwing himself down onto the grate of the floor furnace. He sighed with pleasure as the welcome heat began to thaw him out.

Screaming suddenly, Eddie's whole body seemed to be thrust straight up 'as if he had been levitated by a mischievous poltergeist. He then slammed back onto the floor and began to roll all the while slapping at his smoking ass. Moaning...He rolled over onto his stomach and then we could see what had happened.

The super heated grate of the floor furnace had reacted to his frozen jeans and the numbed cheeks of his butt and burned a perfect checkerboard pattern through his Levi's and into the cheeks of his big blubber butt.

Eddie wouldn't allow Cissy to look at his butt, so Volta, James and I had to do the doctoring. Cissy made us a poultice of cornstarch and lard which seemed to soothe him as we brushed it onto his bright red ass with a basting brush from her kitchen. Eddie rode bare assed, face down in the back seat of Volta's car all the way home to Silver City Courts. We didn't see or hear from him for several days.

By the time Eddie returned to school, everybody knew about the brand on his ass, and being allowed to see it became a status symbol. Boys got to see it in gym, and girls got to take a look by passing the bushes of the pit where Eddie would moon them "by request."

I don't give a fuck what your Momma says, them crazy people is dangerous." Ms. Birdsong was organizing a Christmas program for the State Hospital and I had been badgering Eddie to volunteer along with me. I thought it might be our chance for stardom. Eddie was having second thoughts.

"No they ain't, Momma says they're just pitiful. Besides, they keep the dangerous ones locked up in strait jackets."

"How'd you like to stay up late,
like the Islanders do ?

*Wait for Santa to sail in
with your presents in a canoe ?"*

Finally, I was able to get him to agree by offering rehearsal evenings at my house. We ate and laughed a lot, even talked on the phone a lot, but it seemed like we did very little actual rehearsing. We didn't have any accompaniment, so we had a hard time staying together. And, about every time we'd really get going he'd think of some reason to stop. Calling someone, or going to pee.

Momma looked very nice in her starched uniform with her white hose and shoes. She stood watching the proceedings from the far back wall of the cafeteria as the patients were escorted or wheeled in for the performance.

The audience was in all states of dress, from nice dresses with corsages to open back hospital gowns. The patients had been served a fancy Christmas dinner, received small gifts furnished by the State, and now were being brought in and settled down for our program.

Ms. Birdsong blew her pitch pipe, and the show began. The choir attempted several times to get the patients involved in a sing along, but it was a dismal failure. Then it was time for the featured performers. I was sick from anticipation when our turn approached. I don't know whether it was because Momma was there, or because the audience were all strangers, (some very strange). Who knows?

We both wore white shirts, red neck ties, and black pants. Nellie had contributed two straw bowlers with red bands and I thought we looked swell.

Ms. Birdsong asked the musical question:

"How'd you like to spend Christmas on Christmas Island?" And we began:

The minute we started it was clear that not only did Eddie not remember the words, but we simply were not singing very well together. Rather than obviously stumbling over the words Eddie was attempting to make little sounds, synchronizing them if possible with the words I was singing. A cappella is not easy!

I attempted to get my eyes to blur, not wanting to be able to find faces in the audience, especially Momma's or Ms. Birdsong's.

At the musical interlude one of the patients on the front row stood up and began glaring in our direction. Whether she was swaying to the music or was weaving in anger we'll never know.

She began to slowly move towards where we were standing, and apparently no one but Eddie or me had noticed her. The closer she got to us, the faster we sang, until finally the words became one long

If-you-ever-spend-Christmas-on-Christmas-island-you-will-never-stray-for-every-day-your-Christmas-dreams-come-true.

By the time the Nurses and the aides had gotten to her, it was much too late. She had already stepped out of her gown and begun to pee. In an attempt to get away from the splash Eddie stumbled backwards over some chairs and fell to the floor, taking Ms. Birdsong and two thirds of the girls trio with him.

The ensuing shocked quiet slowly gave way to a roar of laughter and a little bit of quiet applause, during which Eddie and I rapidly headed towards the exit without taking our bows.

Perhaps the road to stardom was too hard, or perhaps Eddie wasn't serious about being a star. Either way I felt like just saying "Piss on it."

Christmas and the first of the year came and went, and before we were even aware of the changes, the "Ides of March" and the election for senior class and student body officers were suddenly upon us. Wherever we went, Eddie and I were very vocal about the need to elect James and not to vote for his opponent M.J. Priest.

Also, whenever Eddie or I were around M.J.'s campaign signs seemed to disappear, mysteriously. Anyhow, when the ballots were counted, James won.

"Wilson, have you ever really gotten any?"

"Hell naw, have you?"

"Naw, but Carolee promised that she'll let me do it after the spring sock-hop."

"Shit, she ain't gonna let you do nuthin'!"

"Yes she is if I can learn to dance good!"

We were playing through on the 3rd hole of the Burns Park miniature golf course. James had recently got a job there and when it was slow he would let us play a few rounds in exchange for helping him rake the leaves off the carpeted holes, or for handing out balls and clubs to the paying customers.

Sometimes he even let us take his car, an awful green forty-nine Ford Volta had given him, to go and cruise Snappy's until he got off from work. Eddie never got a license since they didn't have a car, so I got to drive!

J.W. would even let me drive the car to school on one of his and Momma's off days, either Wednesday or Thursday.

On those mornings I'd pick Eddie up first, and then we'd go get Jewel. Then, after dropping Janice off at Junior High we'd go on to the doghouse and drink a coke before school started.

"Jewel and I can teach you to dance real good."

"You reckon she'd do it?"

"Sure, let's ask her."

"Jim dandy on a submarine,
Got a message from a mermaid queen,
She was tangled in a fishing line,
Jim Dandy didn't waste no time.
Go Jim Dandy, Go Jim Dandy, Go."

"Right leftright, left rightleft one twothree one twothree" Eddie lumbered around Jewel's living room floor.

We had moved the couch and chairs back and were trying to give him a little rhythm.

Eddie was sandwiched between us, Jewel in front and me bringing up the rear. Mike sat in the kitchen smoking playing solitaire and watching us.

"Y'all look like fools." said Mike.

"I'll fool your skinny ass if you don't leave us alone." Jewel replied.

"I'm gonna tell Momma you cussed."

"Go ahead, and I'll tell Momma you was smokin'."

"I ain't never gonna learn this shit if y'all don't shut the fuck up." Eddie whined.

The dance lessons and Eddie's pursuit of Carolee's favor continued. Sometimes he'd seem to be getting it (the dancing that is) and other times it was like he was just beginning.

As far as "getting some," well that, too, was a long way off.

On the Saturday night before Easter Eddie and I walked over the hill and sneaked into the Skyline. The next morning we had promised to go to church with James and his family, but for now we were on our own.

We spent most of our time patrolling the upper balconies looking for acquaintances who might be necking or something else even worse. Whenever we spotted a likely car we'd jump up and down on the bumper, knock on the windows or stick our head in and holler:

"Oooo-weeeeeee. look at y'all."

The whole time Eddie was whistling the theme from "The High and the Mighty."

As we got bored and hungry and after having made ourselves sufficient pains in the ass to everyone, we decided to go on to my house and terrorize Janice and any of her girlfriends who might be there. We found no one at home, so we ate some cold corned beef hash, straight out of the can, and went on to bed.

"Thank God from whom all blessings flow
Thank Him all creatures here below
Thank Him above ye heavenly host,
Thank Father, Son, and Holy Ghost.

Easter was cold and wet, and the sermon at 47th. Street Baptist was way too long. Apparently the tulips and buttercups didn't mind or hadn't noticed the weather. They had burst out of the cold ground, and made their annual Easter appearance just a few days earlier.

Eddie and I had ridden to church in the Ford with James where we were met by Cissy and Volta D. Cissy had bribed us into going to church by offering us Easter Dinner. Eddie was never too eager for church, but a meal was another thing, especially a meal as good as Cissy's. He fidgeted all through the sermon, but finally it was over and we were on our way to James's house. This time we followed Cissy and Volta in their brand new Oldsmobile.

"I'm gonna git me some next week" Eddie bragged.

"You ain't gonna git nothin but your fuckin hand ! Never!."

"It ain't right for y'all to talk that way on Sunday."

"Fuck you Knowland" said Eddie as James pulled the Ford into the driveway.

Cissy had baked a ham with all the trimmings, and my favorite, pecan pie. The meal as usual was very good and also very plentiful. As soon as Eddie finished a third helping of everything and James changed out of his church clothes, we headed on to my house for Eddie and me to slip into our jeans.

Cruising Snappy's wasn't particularly satisfying that day, there was hardly anyone there.

"Where's everybody at?" I hollered at Milton as we passed him in his Daddy's pickup.

They're all out at Blue Hole I think." he answered.

On the south side of Little Rock many water-filled pits left over from the mining of bauxite (the ore that aluminum is made from) dot the landscape. Collectively called "Blue Holes," because of the minerals leeching into the water, these pits are a rich azure blue and completely free of fish and snakes. They are also very, very deep, with no shallows. Once in the water you either had to swim, tread water, cling to the rocky sides, or drown.

Kids usually began swimming in these pits around Easter Sunday regardless of the temperature. The more conventional swimming areas, like Willow Springs and Lake Nixon, didn't open until late May, right before High School graduation, and just in time for the senior picnics.

As James's old ford reached the peak of the small hill and started its descent toward the rocky pits, the sun was just beginning to creep out of the low-hanging gray sky. We could see that there were already several cars, and lots of teenagers on the bluffs surrounding the blue, figure eight shaped pits.

"Look, there's Ferrell and M.J."

James was always going off to shake hands or talk to people, and immediately heading off towards the other boys he suddenly left Eddie and me on our own.

Some of the kids were couples, but most were like us, groups of singles.

"Don't be cruel.

to a heart that's true,

I don't want no other love,

Baby it's still you I'm thinking of"

"I think Elvis Presley is a creep, don't you?"

I didn't respond since I had just recently begun greasing my hair into a pompadour and sweeping it to one side, and was doing everything I could to get my sideburns to grow.

"Hey Wilson, you and Eddie want a RC?"

To our left were Herman and his younger brothers Kenneth and Freddy in their daddy's big Buick. What they sometimes lacked in a house, they made up for in the size of their cars.

Herman and I had been in every single class together since the third grade, with Kenneth and Freddy in the next two grades behind us.

A pasty white kid with jet black hair, Herman was just a younger version of his dad. Kenneth was blond and very handsome though and so was Freddy. When he was only ten Freddy had lost a leg to cancer and the stump was a constant source of horrified fascination to everyone, including me.

We took the RC's Herman offered, and Eddie quickly guzzled his and threw the empty bottle into an arc out over the pit.

"Jist look over there at them Moody's. They ain't nothin but common trash. Momma says they owe everybody in town, and that their daddy ain't nuthin but a drunkard."

"You don't know shit about them people Herman, and neither does your Momma."

"I do too, my Momma used to work at the Bakery with their Momma."

"My Momma still does, and she likes Miz Moody."

"Well, I still know what I know, and I got my opinion."

"Bite me shit face."

Frank and Helen Moody along with several other kids from the country were sitting in Frank's pickup drinking something that looked a lot like beer.

Barbara Hartnett, Rosie Sheldon, Julia Dorsett and several other girls had built a fire on a large rock overhang, and were roasting weenies on straightened coat hangers.

Several of the more daring kids were jumping into the water, but it was too cold for me, and I was always a little afraid of swimming in these holes, anyway.

"Hey George, do you want a hotdog?"

"Sure Barb, thanks"

Eddie and the others hooted and whistled as I walked over to the fire. I shot them a finger for their trouble. I always felt a little shy around these girls. Barbara and Rosie were cheerleaders, and the others were popular or we thought they were rich.

I polished off a couple of hot-dogs, and Rosie turned up the car radio. The flat rock formed a natural dance surface and she and Julia began to dance together. Barbara took my hand and we began to dance. Slow!

"I found my thrill on blueberry hill,
On blueberry hill when I found you.
The moon stood still on blueberry hill,
And lingered until my dreams came true"

"Are you gonna try out for the junior play?"

"I dunno."

"You ought to. Everybody thinks you'd get it."

"I don't even know what it's about."

"It's about a ghost."

It seemed as if everyone except me wanted me in the play. I was more self confident than before, but what if I didn't get it? What if I got it and was awful?

Barbara had shown up at the Dog house with the script one day, and after I read a few lines it seemed as if it had been written just for me. I began to see myself in the part. Not just saying the lines, but really being the character. I also began to see the kids who were listening, smiling, accepting, even applauding.

If there was ever a time in my life when I was the person to beat it was during tryouts for the play.

It wasn't who would get the part, but who would get the other parts. There was a boy named Franklin who thought, incorrectly, that he was going to give me a run for the money.

The auditions were closed, but I told Eddie I could get him in. He said no.

"I ain't goin' to tryouts for no sissy play."

I read first with Pat and Kenneth, (the favorites for the other major roles). And, after Franklin read with them, the drama teacher announced that I would play "Inner Willie" (as expected), but that she would like for Franklin to play Willie.

After these roles were cast, we read the lines with each of the other groups as the parts of the mother, the father, and the sister were cast.

Both the junior play "Brainstorm" and the senior play "Twelve angry men" were in May, just about two weeks apart. The night of the play Momma, J.W., Betty Jo, Neecy and Barbara (we had been going steady since Blue Hole) all sat together.

"Inner Willie, the alter ego" (my character) was visible only to Willie (the main character) and the audience.

Wearing bright pink long johns, I crawled over the furniture, lounged on the piano, and pranced all over the stage, all the while doing the tricks only recently learned with a bright pink yo-yo.

At first the audience seemed startled by my appearance, but after they got into it, it became a romp. I could even see my reserved Momma laughing out loud.

When the curtain came down, the applause was tremendous, and when I took my bow I received a standing ovation. What a thrill!

The cast party afterwards was at the new youth center, and after telling Momma and them bye, Barbara and I slowly walked the two blocks holding hands and talking.

"Love…yea yea, love is strange. uh-huh,
lots of people yea yea, take it for a game"
Mickey and Sylvia heralded our entrance.

The place was about half full, most of the kids dancing the Cha-lypso, and a few small scattered groups standing or sitting, drinking soft drinks.

Eddie and James were sitting side by side on the floor with their backs against the wall watching the action. They didn't return my wave, but probably they just hadn't seen me.

"Hey Eddie, Hey James."

"Hey big shit, you shore are getting stuck up."

"I ain't stuck up."

"You think your shit don't stink."

"Fuck you Eddie." And I turned away.

I walked back over to where Barbara and the rest of the cast were waiting, and I barely noticed when Eddie and James left. He had been acting funny ever since I started dating Barbara. It was like it was okay for him to chase around after Carolee, but I had just better not have a girlfriend. What did he expect, I was getting popular, and kids were beginning to like me.

It was only about two weeks until summer vacation, and there were a whole lot of activities planned, and lots of things to do.

Eddie and I hadn't seen much of each other since that night at the Youth Center, and the few times we had seen each other, he still seemed to be pissed off at me.

Well, I hadn't done anything to him, and as they say, "Pissed off is better than pissed on!"

The seniors were always given the day off, but it was always understood that the juniors skipped school and crashed the senior picnic at Willow Springs.

Only the sophomores were expected to be in class the day of the picnic.

Summer arrives suddenly in Arkansas. One day it's spring, cool and breezy, and the world smells of flowers and mist. The very next morning the heat is stifling, there's not a breeze stirring anywhere, and the sweat courses right down into the crack of your ass.

This was one of those days.

The huge covered dance floor overlooked the lake with its slides and the two large diving platforms built in the center of the water.

They were used mostly for sun-bathing rather than diving, but the rumor was that after dark the platforms were used for other things because the colored lights of the dance pavilion were too dim to reach that far.

During previous summers Eddie and I had noticed necking, and kids laying real close on the platforms.

A couple of times Eddie and me were fairly sure that hands had been slipped into the top of girls swimsuits, or into a boys bathing trunks for a little feel.

Everyone had on new swimsuits or Cabana outfits. Barbara and I rode with Julia and Kenneth in his new convertible. Eddie and Carolee had ridden with James who was with that fat-ass Anita Stockard. Outweighing James by at least a hundred pounds, you would think that the recently elected Vice President of the entire student body would have been able to do a lot better if he would just try.

The others cleared a space for Barbara and me as we began to dance. We had really gotten to be pretty good...lots of practice I guess.

Barbara taught me lots of new steps and several new dances, which I shared with Eddie and Jewel. During these impromptu dance lessons, I discovered that not only was I able to learn, and improve on what I had learned. I was also able to teach.

Jewel had been going steady with the senior, Jackie Morris since Christmas, and it looked like they'd probably get married. Everybody said they were doing it, but Jewel denied it.

Lunch was cold rubbery Hamburgers and bags of potato chips. Iced tea or lemonade was in the big old 50 gallon drums with spigots on the side. I knew I would be able to find Eddie near the food.

"You and Carolee ain't dancin'?" It was more of a statement than a question.

"Naw, she's got her period."

"I reckon that's good news, specially, if y'all are doing it."

"Dipshit" followed by his punch on my shoulder was all the answer I needed.

"I knew you wasn't gettin any."

"George honey, what you doin?" Barbara whined. "C'mon and let's go swim and cool off."

"Georgy honey, you better go cool off now." Eddie mocked.

We ran into the already warm waters of the lake, and began to swim out to the largest platform. As we looked back over our shoulders we had a panoramic view of the sandy shore and the dance pavilion. Kenneth and Bobby were holding Rosie's wrists, trying to grab her ankles with their free hands.

Finally succeeding the boys began to swing her back and forth stomach down, and with her head facing the lake. As she reached the top of an arc they released her and she flew chest first out into the lake. Slamming down into the water, Rosie made a terrific splash, and standing up and laughing, she turned around to make her way back to the shore.

There was a huge gasp from the girls on shore, and then the boys began to crack up. Rosie hit the water with such force that it ripped the strap off her one piece swimsuit and the top had folded back almost to her waist. Her more than ample boobs were now completely exposed and hung towards the water. Suddenly realizing what had happened, Rosie screamed.

With one motion she lifted the suit, and folded it and her hands over her breasts, falling face first sobbing onto the sand.

It took the other cheerleaders several minutes before they were able to convince her to stay. Of course It took substantially longer however for the guys to stop laughing and talking about what they'd seen and before our attentions were drawn elsewhere.

"THERE WILL BE A DANCE CONTEST AT 2:30" crackled from the loudspeakers.

"Wanta enter the contest?"

"Naw." I was sure not gonna compete. At least not yet.

"Aw, why not? "

"Emily and Gary are gonna win."

"How do you know? Mr. Smarty britches."

"Cause they're the best dancers in school."

"Well, you might be surprised if you'd just give yourself a

chance."

"Aw Barb, leave me alone."

"GRAB YOUR PARTNERS. THE CONTEST STARTS IN 15 MINUTES."

"Come on George."

"I told you no!"

"I'll get some one else."

"Well, go on then."

"THE TOP THREE COUPLES WILL BE SPOTLIGHT DANCERS
ON THE 5 OCLOCK HOP!"

"Aw come on honey, I'd love to be on the Hop."

"Well, I guess it wouldn't hurt nothin' to try." The chance for fame and some public recognition held too strong an appeal.

Eddie and Carolee were eliminated in the first wave, along with James and Anita.

There were four dances in the contest, the cha-lypso, the jitterbug, a slow dance (we always did lots of dipping) and a second jitterbug.

The strains of "Let it be me" began and Barbara and I slowly began moving around the floor.

"I bless the day I found you,
I want to stay around you,
Now and forever, let it be me.
Don't take this heaven from one,
When you must cling to someone,
Now and forever let it be me"

As couple after couple was eliminated, the audience began cheering loudly for their favorites.

"Go Emily."

"All right Wilson!"

"Gary, Gary, Gary."

"Yea Barbara."

As we entered the final dance, the jitterbug, there were only five couples left.

"You know I can be found,
Sittin' home all alone,
If you can't come around,
At least please telephone,
Don't be cruel, to a heart that's true"
Barbara twirled under my arm, swung around and back under and we started our move across the dance floor. *1,2,3-1,2,3, left and back. 1,2,3,-1,2,3, left and back.*

Stepping forward I began swinging her backwards all the while holding her left shoulder snugly with my right hand. The swing felt right, and she winked as I caught her eye.

"Baby if I made you mad,
Somethin that I might have said
Please just forget the past,
The future looks bright ahead.
Don't be cruel, to a heart that's true. "
Another elimination, and now there were only four couples left.
"Wilson, Wilson, Wilson."
"Come on Jackie."
"Tear em up Em."

We survived the next elimination, but Jewel and Jackie were eliminated, and now there were just three couples;

Gary and Emily, Barbara and I, and Arlis Rainey and her brother Denny, who was also a junior.

"As I was a motivatin over the hill
I saw Maybelline in a Coupe De Ville
A spotlight on the Hop…I could think of little else as we entered the final competition.

The dance ended without any further elimination. There was a smattering of confused applause and then almost complete silence as we stood waiting on the smooth plank floor.

I still don't remember hearing the announcement that we had won second place, because when Arlis and Denny were announced as third place my heart had completely stopped.

Of course Gary and Emily were first!

The kids went wild, and there was suddenly a huge crowd on the dance floor that only seconds ago had been almost empty.

Everyone was crowding around, hugging the girls and patting the boy's shoulders, and sometimes, even shaking hands in their eagerness to congratulate each other. Eddie had congratulated me, even giving me a thumb up. He and Carolee had even sat with Barbara and me for a few minutes as the Picnic was wound down.

"I hope you ain't plannin' on wearin' them sissy blue suede shoes out in public!"

"Yes fat fuck, I am wearing them! Everybody's wearin' them."

"Not everybody,…I ain't."

"Well, that's just because"…and suddenly, blessedly without saying something I shouldn't have, I bit my tongue.

Eddie and I had made up, and were at Rephan's buying me an outfit for the "Hop."

I also got a pink shirt, a pink suede belt, and with blue jeans and the blue suede shoes I was bound to be a standout.

Barbara wore a blue blouse, a collar dyed to match her pink skirt, and T strap ballerinas. Her blonde hair was combed into a bustle back, and I combed and greased mine into a perfect Elvis Presley DA.

The day of the hop was July the second and since him and Momma were off work, J.W. agreed to let me use the Chevy. After I picked up Eddie, we drove over to Barbara's house to get her and Carolee. They were using the extra passes that had been given to each of the spotlight dancers.

We were allowed to enter through a special door, while Eddie, Carolee and the other kids had to wait on the sidewalk.

It was a typical July day in Little Rock. Steaming hot without even a hint of a breeze, sweat was coursing down Eddie's face and Carolee's armpits had made huge damp circles on her yellow sweater. Even the nylon scarf around her neck was damp and wilting.

"Smart ass" Eddie mumbled as Barbara and I passed and entered the air conditioned darkness of Channel 4.

The center of the dark studio was burned away by the bright lights on the set. It glowed incandescent in the middle of cable, wire, machinery and people. The three spotlighted couples were assigned small elevated circles where we would dance.

"We'll be opening with a fast song, "*Book of Love*" and next will be "*Love is a Many Splendored Thing.*" Then we'll close with a chalypso to "*Little Darlin.*"

"Y'all OK with that?"

Jay Crockett was the emcee, and he looked all right on TV but in person he looked like a Kewpie doll. His lips and cheeks were rouged, and his red hair looked like a Nazi helmet.

This was the first time I had seen a man in makeup.

The doors opened and the other kids rushed in trying to position themselves on the floor in front of the featured dancers so that they might get a chance to be on camera. Eddie and Carolee muscled their way through the crowd until they were directly below us.

The theme began;

One, two, three, o'clock four o'clock rock.

Five, six, seven, o'clock eight o'clock rock.

Nine, ten, eleven o'clock twelve o'clock rock.

We're gonna rock around the clock tonight.

All the kids crowded the floor making it difficult for us to do any of our more intricate moves, but I still noticed that at least one of the cameras never left me and Barbara.

The first selection began

"well I wonder, wonder, who,

googy do wop, who, who wrote the book of love

As the lights dimmed, a spotlight began to follow us as we moved across our small private circle.

While the circle wasn't very large, there were no walls or other kids, so we were really able to get some great movements going in the little area.

It seemed way too brief! The spotlight was moved to each of the other couples in turn, and then returned to us for a very short time before the song ended. For the next song, (the slow one) I let Barbara enter the spotlight alone, where after just a second I extended my hand into the circle of light, and taking it she spun right into me before we began our dance. Barely moving, it worked out perfectly for me to dip her way back as the music crescendo-ed and the spotlight moved to the next couple. Fabulous!

We also started the Cha-lypso apart. Dancing to each other from across the floor the audience began applauding wildly. We had recently learned to breakaway, where turning your partner away from you, still holding her hand, you dance, side by side.

American Bandstand my Ass!

"Yes son, we saw you on TV, and y'all looked real nice." Momma and J.W. had invited the neighbors over to watch with them and Janice and when we got home there was still quite a crowd waiting to see us.

After a few more congratulations and a few requests for lessons folks went on back home leaving just Eddie and us. We had driven the girls' home first and then gone on to my house to eat supper. Momma was never much of a cook, but there was always plenty, and it was always hot.

As usual, the food was salty, cooked in lard or bacon drippings, and it was tender. This worked better for Eddie than it did for me or my sisters. Quality never seemed to be too much of a problem for Eddie, because he was always a great deal more interested in quantity.

Taking two more slices of light bread, after slathering them with margarine, he asked;

"Did y'all see me and Carolee too?"

"We sure did, yawl was right in front of Sonny and Barbara."

"Momma, call me George, Sonny's a kid name!"

"Yes George! Is that better."

Momma didn't like to be sassed or corrected, but this time she let it pass. Maybe it was because I was growing up, and had been on television and all. But, she still gave me one of her looks.

"Wanna walk over to the youth center after supper?" I asked.

"Sure" Eddie replied talking around a mouth stuffed with potatoes and cream gravy.

"Hon, you boys can take my Hudson if you want to." This from Betty.

Sister Jo had arrived back in Little Rock from Fallbrook, just a few weeks after me. It turned out that Adam and the marriage had both been very bad ideas. According to her, he was more interested in playing soldier, and running with his buddies than he had been in their relationship.

She had retrieved the babies from the nuns with little apparent damage, and all three were now back living with us.

As soon as Eddie finished eating we got in the old Hudson and headed on down to the dance at the Youth Center. It was Friday night, and the holiday weekend had already started by the time Eddie and I had parked the Hudson.

Most of the football team, a few of their cheerleader girlfriends and their ever present second string cronies were outside of the center setting off fireworks. Throwing firecrackers and cherry bombs at anyone within tossing distance, they were being general pains in the ass. Eddie and I fell right in along with them.

This was a place where several years before I would not have been welcome, or comfortable. Eddie had introduced me to this! He had made me feel accepted. He had let me know, finally, that it was enough just to be me. My recent popularity from the play and the Spotlight dance might have been enough. But, who knows?

"Owww, Fuck me!" The quarterback Jeff Deresaw howled as a ladyfinger firecracker he had intended for Eddie detonated in his hand.

"Aw, sweetie, let me kiss it for you." whined Melba, his gorgeous but fairly simple steady girlfriend.

"Oh Melba baby you can kiss mine too...when you're through with Deresaw's." said Robby Turner, the fullback, grabbed his crotch and fell back.

Everyone, even the more reserved girls laughed out loud.

"Eddie honey, y'all wait for me!" Carolee screeched from the top of the small but very steep hill that sloped down to the youth center.

"Fuck me" moaned Eddie "I thought she was gonna stay home."

Carolee was much too fond of purple, and this evening her full skirt, her cotton blouse with the turned up collar, her bobby socks and even the nylon scarf tied around her ponytail were all the color of an overripe 200 pound eggplant. Even the fucking Mary-Janes were purple.

Waddling just a few steps behind her was Anita similarly dressed, except for the color. Anita had chosen a somewhat electric orange outfit. Even their clutch bags (held tightly in their fat little hands) were perfect matches.

The word clash was invented for the picture these two made, leaning back in an effort to compensate for the slope of the hill, trying hard not to appear clumsy. They chose their footings very carefully as they cautiously descended, and in perfect unison and step.

Unobserved in the quickly descending dusk Robby managed to circle around behind them, and still unnoticed he rolled a lit cherry bomb onto the sidewalk directly under Anita's orange skirt.

KaBoom...

Through the puff of blue smoke we could see Anita's skirt and her crinolines being blown upwards, exposing her ample thighs and her bloomers (also orange).

Stepping forward, fanning both hands in front of her face, her pursed lips made small "oooing sounds." Then she toppled sideways over onto the ground in a dead faint.

"Now see what y'all have done...Y'all are so hateful!"

Carolee was mad...

"Eddie, stop your laughing, this ain't funny."

"George Wilson goddammit she's hurt, stop that fucking laughing."

"I'm gonna tell Mr. Miller on all of y'all."

"Chromedome can't do a fucking thang. We ain't at school" (Mr. Miller was the completely bald principal at NLR High School)

By the time Carolee was able to revive Anita by spitting onto her handkerchief and then laying it across Anita's forehead we had only barely stopped laughing. Anita regained her composure and after calling us a bunch of "sons of bitches." tromped off to the bathroom with Carolee in tow to make some badly needed repairs.

We hung around outside the Youth center for a while longer. Then, tiring of that, we went inside and after awhile Carolee had forgiven Eddie for laughing, and they had danced a few dances together. Mostly I had just hung out making fun of or talking about the other kids. The dance was over around ten, so we got into the Hudson and headed back towards Levy.

"We gonna go to the Skyline tomorrow night?" Eddie asked.

"Naw, I'm gonna go eat with Barbara and her Momma."

"You ought to let that fuckin' Barbara adopt you, you act like her little boy."

"I don't either. But what about you and Carolee? You're always running around sniffing at her butt, like some mangy old dog in heat."

"You have really got to where you think your shit don't stink since you was in that fucking play."

"Yeah, well at least I ain't wearing no raggedy-assed old letter jacket like it was something important. And besides, who asked you for your fucking opinion anyhow?

Instead of making the turn towards Levy at Railroad Avenue, I crossed the tracks and headed towards the Courts. I was so fucking mad I didn't want him at my house. He realized instantly what I was doing, and at the first stop sign he threw open the door, and slamming it behind him said:

"Fuck you, asshole."

As he headed out towards the Courts I pulled back onto Railroad and headed on out to Fiftieth Street.

"Who needed him telling me what the shit to do anyhow?"

All day Saturday I waited for Eddie to call and apologize. I sure as shit wasn't going to apologize to him! After all, he had started it, hadn't he? A couple of times I almost called to give him a chance to make amends, but I wasn't going to kiss his ass. I had plenty of other friends.

Besides, it really was more than just supper at Barbara's. She had invited some of the other cheerleaders and their boyfriends, and after eating we were all gonna dance to the radio, or maybe have a sing-along as she played the piano.

"Sonny, will you give me and Virgie a ride to the Skyline on your way to Barbara's?" Janice asked.

She and her best girlfriend had spent Friday night at our house, and most of Saturday hanging off the phone, or talking about boys and giggling. I just hated kids.

"That's out of my way!"

"Son, if you're gonna use the car, you can just take the girls to the picture show first, okay?"

"I guess so Momma." And, that was the end of that.

"How y'all gonna get to Virgies after the show hon?" Momma asked.

"We can get a ride with someone or we'll walk."

"That'd be a mighty long walk, Janice. Y'all call if you can't get a ride and maybe Sonny will be home and me and J.W. will come get you."

"Okay Momma."

"It was just getting dark as I let Janice and Virgie out in Levy.

"Momma said you was taking us to the show."

"Well, this is as close as I'm going, I'm almost late now." I said, speeding off and leaving them in front of the drugstore.

The party was everything I wanted it to be. Hal was even there with his new girlfriend, and he had recently got a letter from Joe. Joe was getting married to a Mexican girl he met in San Diego, and when he got his discharge he promised to bring her back to Arkansas to meet us.

Supper was just sandwiches and things, but it was still lots of fun. We started in at the piano even before we ate, and the dancing went on right through the meal. Some of the kids even danced to the piano while the rest of us sang.

Barbara and I were the best dancers there, and whenever we'd get up, they'd clear a place on the living room floor for us. Sometimes there was even applause.

Virgie and Janice had gotten up to go to the bathroom leaving their seats in front of the concession stand. Starting back out the door Virgie ran headfirst into Tommy.

"Hey Tommy."

"Hey Virgie. Who you here with?"

"Oh just me and Janice, who are you with?"

"Eddie, and James, we came in James's car, who'd y'all come with."

As Janice exited the bathroom she said: "Sonny dropped us off, you reckon James, would give us a ride out to Virgie's when the show is over?"

"Shore, why don't y'all come over to the car and make sure?"

It was a hot night, and James and Eddie were sitting on the hood of the car when Tommy arrived back with the girls in tow.

"James, would you give me and Virgie a ride out to her house when the shows over?" Janice asked.

"Sure." he replied.

"Well, I'm riding in the front seat, and that's final."

"What's new Eddie? You always ride in the front seat." said Virgie.

"Where's George at?" Tommy asked as they approached Virgie's house.

"He and Barbara had a party over at her house." answered Janice.

"He didn't tell me they was having a fuckin' party!"

"Eddie you are the nastiest talking thing, I wish you'd learn how to act."

"Thanks for the ride James. Goodnight Tommy." The girls said ignoring Eddie as they stepped from the car. He was just too outrageous.

James turned the car around, started back down east Third Street, and they headed towards town.

"Can't you get anything but that old hillbilly shit on the radio?" Eddie reached out and played with the knobs as James dealt with the gear shift and Tommy spoke up from the back seat:

"That Janice Wilson is sure cute."

"You'd think anything but your right hand is cute."

"This piece of shit radio don't have no stations, James."

"Oh Eddie, you just don't know how to work it."

'Yeah, well work it your ownself goddammit."

As James leaned over the radio he was unaware that his foot continued to press down on the accelerator. He squinted at the numbers on the back-lighted dial and lifted his head just in time, suddenly jerking the steering wheel hard to the left.

Eddie was still bent over the radio, and never saw the disabled truck blocking the right lane.

"Honey…wake up."

"Huh?"

"Oh, George honey, wake up. Somethin' awful has happened."

"What?"

"James had a car wreck and Eddie's dead…"

"Huh?"

"The police want to know if you know where Eddie's folks are at in Brinkley."

"Betty, is this a joke?"

"No Honey, it's the truth. Monte Montgomery called me." Monte was now the Captain of the North Little Rock police force.

"It ain't the truth. He can't be dead."

"Oh, Sonny."

"They made a mistake. He ain't dead. Who said he's dead?"

"Hon, they're at Baptist Hospital."

"Take me there."

On the way to the hospital Betty said Monte had told her that they had hit a parked truck on East Broadway, and that Eddie had died on the street.

It couldn't be possible. I had never known anyone who died, and Eddie was not dead. It was all a mistake, and someone else was dead, maybe James, but not Eddie. Oh, please God, not Eddie.

When we arrived at the hospital, Betty rushed in and I hung slightly back not wanting to hear what they might have to say in this awful place.

The corridor at the hospital was cold and empty except for the stooped black man passing his dirty rancid mop in ever diminishing circles.

"No, we don't have an Eddie Rice."

"Do you have a James Knowland then?" Betty asked.

Shuffling through the register she said "Yes, ma'am. He's in the emergency room."

Cissy sat with her head buried in her hands, and Volta D. was standing, with a Camel in his leathery brown fingers.

"Thanks for coming George. Did you know how to reach the Rice's in Brinkley?"

"No, how's Eddie?"

"Didn't they tell you, George?" asked Volta. "Eddies dead."

Cissy began to sob quietly as Betty slowly sank onto the plastic sofa and covered her eyes.

"Are they sure? Have the Doctors said so for sure? "

"Oh George, they tried everything they could, but he died on the curb where they had the wreck before the ambulance could even get there."

"What happened, Mrs. Corcoran?" asked Sister Jo.

"James and Eddie were at the Skyline with Tommy and when the show was over they gave Janice and Virgie Kilgore a ride home."

"Oh my God" cried Betty "Was Janice hurt?"

"No, they had already let them out at Virgie's and were on their way back when they hit a truck that was broke down in the road."

"Oh, thank God, was James or Tommy hurt?"

"James has a broken nose, and they both got a few cuts."

"George, are you all right?"

"George!"

"Huh?"

"Are you all right?"

"I guess so, Sister. Lets go home now."

"Don't you want to see James?"

Cissy asked as I turned away and started slowly back down the corridor. Not answering, I walked towards the door and out of this sterile smelling place. I wanted to see my friend! Not my dead friend, but my live friend. Where was Eddie? If he were here he'd know what to do.

Later, we would learn that the impact had driven the dashboard back into Eddie's chest. He was gasping for breath with blood pouring from his mouth, when the driver of the truck and James pulled him from the car.

I didn't speak as we drove to Virgie's house to pick up Neecy. I couldn't think of anything to say. Maybe if we didn't talk about it, it wouldn't be true. Maybe it would go away if I didn't acknowledge its existence. I had to think of a way to make it not true...

"Why Betty Jo, what's wrong?"

"There's been an accident Mrs. Kilgore and we need to pick up Janice."

"What's happened?" "Is anyone hurt?"

"Eddie Rice is dead!"

"Oh my God, let me wake the girls."

Neecy wiped her eyes as she slowly walked into the room...

"What is it, Sister Jo?"

"James had a wreck after they let you out last night, and Eddie was killed."

Neecy let out a loud scream, and sobbed pitifully as we walked to Betty's old Hudson. Only after several minutes of hugging and patting was Sister Jo able to get her calmed down enough to be allowed to turn the car around and head back towards Levy. As the dawn of Independence Day burned through the night, the sky burst into streaks of amber and turquoise mingled with green. The hollow disbelief now turning slowly into immeasurable grief seemed to be mocking this spectacularly beautiful holiday morning.

"Happy Fourth of July! Have a wonderful day America!" blared the old Hudson's radio...

The song of love is a sad song,. Hi lili...,Hi lili, ...Hi lo,
The song of love is a song of woe, don't ask me how I know.
The song of love is a sad song, for I have loved and it's true.
I sit at my window and watch the rain, Hi lili,...Hi lili...Hi low.
Tomorrow I'll probably love again.

Somehow I was able to get through the rest of Sunday. Family and friends came and went. I was offered and usually declined food or drink. I believe Barbara was there, but I'm not sure. I do remember being told that the funeral was to be in Brinkley on Monday.

I do remember the fireworks though. As if in macabre celebration of the horror, everywhere seemed to be alive with explosion or whistles. Why couldn't there be silence? Didn't they know someone had died?

The rapidly warming air of Monday morning beat relentlessly into our faces through the vent windows of the Hudson, giving us little relief from the heat or the heartbreak.

Jewel, in pink dotted Swiss, stood alone waiting on her front porch when the Hudson pulled up for the long trip to Brinkley.

Silent in the backseat, I refused to believe where I was going and why. We were on our way to bury my best friend, perhaps my only friend.

How was I ever going to be able to face Nellie? Eddies family had not returned to North Little Rock, but his daddy had come in to identify Eddie's body.

What did it mean to identify a body? Didn't they know for sure that it was him? If he had to be identified, maybe it wasn't him. Maybe someone had made a mistake.

"I ain't gonna go in." These were the first words I had spoken since we left Little Rock.

"Now Hon, we need to go in and see Eddie's Momma and them."

"Oh Sister Jo, I can't, I just can't" and the long hidden tears now slowly began. "Yawl go on in."

"I'm stayin' here with Sonny." Neecy laid her head on my shoulder.

Jewel and Betty stepped out of the Hudson leaving me and Neecy alone in the back seat.

"Oh Sonny, I'm so sorry, it's all my fault! If Virgie and I hadn't asked James for a ride this wouldn't have happened."

She began to sob.

uhwwww, ohhhhh, sniff "Eddie *uhhh wahhh* let a big stinky poot when we got to Virgie's, and I said Eddie Rice, *sniff, sniff* I just hate you."

I was so intent on watching her that I hadn't noticed Nellie had come out of her Mother's house with Betty and Jewel.

"Oh George, please give me a hug, I can't do this without you here. You and me loved him the most."

I couldn't answer…but as Nellie's arms went around me, I put mine around her neck and squeezed as if we might somehow be able to change things.

"Oh, Janice, if only he had gotten out of the car with you." Nellie said, and once again, Neecy fell on her face and began to wail.

As we entered the dusty red brick church someone handed us small folded papers which had Eddie's name on the front above the date, July 4, 1956. I barely noticed the prayers and songs printed on the inside, and folding it into a tiny square I pressed it tightly into the center of my left fist and held it there. I suppose I hoped that the pressure and the pain would make it and the day disappear.

There were tri-fold paper fans with pictures of *Jesus in the garden* alongside the hymnals in the small wooden racks in front of us. These racks also had little finger-sized holes for used communion glasses. Everyone seemed to be fanning when the family entered.

I had never seen Eddie's Grandmother. She was an older grayer version of Nellie, leaning on her only child's arm as they made their way to the front pew. Next came the four younger boys looking somewhat bewildered, followed closely by Eddie's daddy, who walked alone behind his remaining family. His face looked like gray metal as he followed his four lonely little boys into the wooden pew.

It seemed as if the preacher would never stop talking. He droned on and on, saying things like "ashes to ashes." Why didn't he say something that would change things? Why couldn't he intercede and get his God to reverse the events of the last three days? Why didn't he get him to bring Eddie back long enough for me to at least tell him I was sorry? Why didn't his God take someone else? It didn't have to be Eddie, did it?

I couldn't take my eyes off the rectangular silver box with its lace pillow where Eddie lay, his forehead barely visible.

Silently I spoke to him the whole time, apologizing, asking him to come back, and somehow be there with me once again.

Jewel was on one side of me and Betty sat on the other. They both kept putting their arms around me or their hands on me in a futile attempt at consolation or comfort, but it didn't work, nothing could!

All the while I didn't realize that the loud sniffling sobs were coming from me.

And then it was over. Nellie drew herself up, walked over to the coffin, lay her right arm over Eddie's, stooped, and kissed his lips.

His daddy appeared at her side, and whispering silent words he touched his hand to Eddie's brow. Then slowly, silently they both moved away.

Eddie's Grandmother paused, looking down at him for what seemed like an eternity. Then, she wiped her eyes, and also moved towards the door leaving the other boys standing alone with their big brothers coffin.

Suddenly from halfway towards the door Nellie screamed, "Oh God, give him back to me. Please don't punish me this way!"

Stumbling and falling Nellie pushed her way back to the coffin where she collapsed.

Rock of ages, cleft for me,
Let me hide my self in thee...
Let the water and the blood
From thy wounded side which flowed,
Be of sin the perfect cure...
Free from wrath and make me pure

Nellie's stricken husband and her ashen mother helped her up and once again led her away...followed by four very confused little boys.

The other mourners in front of us slowly stood and began their terrible procession past the coffin. Betty gently took my right arm encouraging me to rise and join the others.

"I ain't gonna go down there."

"You don't wanta tell him bye, son?"

"I ain't goin Sister Jo."

Jewel stood and moved to her left as Betty passed in front of me. I sat still, staring straight ahead, frozen in time.

Only when they had lowered the silver lid into place and began to move the flowers to the hearse was I able to rise and begin moving towards the door.

I hadn't been able to tell my friend good-bye, but I would follow him up the aisle and into the warm summer sunshine.

My sisters and Jewel stood silently watching as the pallbearers gently lifted the coffin down the front stairs of the church, followed by just one lone mourner, his best friend, now a heartbroken young boy.

The road to the cemetery snaked through the flower covered hills of northeast Arkansas, crossing small streams and rivers, and finally through an arch of brick and iron that gave a name to this horrible place.

As the others stepped out of the car I sat still. I wouldn't, I couldn't watch this. They were going to put him in the ground in that small box...forever. There would be no light there. He would be all alone there, with no one who cared.

I could see the small mound of red dirt off to the left, and watched as the six men carried their burden and lowered it gently onto the skirted table.

I could see Nellie and her family as they got out of the black hearse and walked once again to the front of the crowd. But I would never have been able to stand to see my friend put into the ground for eternity.

As the preacher once again began his singsong intonations, I sat in the backseat of the Hudson and unfolded the paper from the church. I read the quotation which was to go on Eddie's headstone, and whose origin I would not learn for many years:

"Farewell Sweet Prince May flights of angels sing thee to thy rest"

Printed in the United States
59355LVS00002B/48